"Please, Monro, leave me alone."

Caitlin spoke wearily. "It's late and I'm tired. I just want to get some sleep."

"Come home with me, then. We can talk in the morning," he said, his voice gentler. "Caitlin, we have to talk if we're going to save our marriage."

She was too distraught to be wary of how she phrased it, she just threw her response at him roughly. "Our marriage is over."

He stared down into her face. "Over?" he repeated dully. "Suddenly our marriage is over without explanation, warning, anything."

"Oh, please just let me go," she said, trying to dart into the house.

He caught her arm, talking thickly. "I'll never let you go, Caitlin. Not in a million years. You're mine, do you hear?"

CHARLOTTE LAMB began to write "because it was one job I could do without having to leave the children." Now writing is her profession. She has had more than forty Harlequin novels published since 1978. "I love to write," she explains, "and it comes very easily to me." She and her family live in a beautiful old home on the Isle of Man, between England and Ireland. Charlotte spends eight hours a day writing—and enjoys every minute of it.

Books by Charlotte Lamb

A VIOLATION
SECRETS

HARLEQUIN PRESENTS

1001—HIDE AND SEEK
1025—CIRCLE OF FATE
1042—KISS OF FIRE
1059—WHIRLWIND
1081—ECHO OF PASSION
1106—OUT OF CONTROL
1170—NO MORE LONELY NIGHTS
1202—DESPERATION
1236—SEDUCTIVE STRANGER
1290—RUNAWAY WIFE
1345—RITES OF POSSESSION

HARLEQUIN ROMANCE

2696—KINGFISHER MORNING
2804—THE HERON QUEST
2950—YOU CAN LOVE A STRANGER

CHARLOTTE LAMB

dark pursuit

Harlequin Books

TORONTO • NEW YORK • LONDON
AMSTERDAM • PARIS • SYDNEY • HAMBURG
STOCKHOLM • ATHENS • TOKYO • MILAN

Harlequin Presents first edition June 1991
ISBN 0-373-11370-6

Original hardcover edition published in 1990
by Mills & Boon Limited

DARK PURSUIT

CHAPTER ONE

CAITLIN was running late that evening, and Monro was going to be angry if she wasn't ready by the time he tapped on her door, so as she moved around her room she kept one eye on the clock. Monro's rage was not something she wanted to provoke.

She had left plenty of time to get ready for this reception at Lydgate House, but when she had gone up to change she had found her step-daughter, Gill, lying in wait for her at the top of the stairs.

'Come and kiss me goodnight!' she had pleaded, hugging Caitlin.

Rumpling the girl's hair and laughing, Caitlin had pretended to be stern. 'I did that an hour ago! Why aren't you asleep?'

'It's too light, and I'm wide awake. Sit and talk to me, tell me a story...oh, please, Caitlin!' A tiny, slightly built child of seven, Gill knew she could twist Caitlin round her little finger. She had her father's dark hair and light grey eyes, although on Gill they had more warmth than Caitlin had ever seen in Monro's eyes. She had, too, a fragility that caught Caitlin's breath.

Tucking Gill back into bed, telling her a story and kissing her goodnight had delayed Caitlin by ten minutes. She had had to hurry after that, but she showed no sign of nerves as she sat in front of her dressing-table mirror, doing her make-up. She had learnt through bitter experience never to reveal what was going on under her cool surface.

Tonight, as usual, she had methodically showered, dressed, piled her long blonde hair on top of her head in a sleek chignon, and pinned it there with a black velvet bow held in place by a diamond clip. Her dress was an elegant Edwardian-style ballgown, with a bodice of black satin striped with silver, the neckline plunging to the deep white hollow between her breasts, the sleeves ballooning to a tight cuff at the wrist. Caitlin was slender enough to wear the very tight waist without discomfort, and she loved the rustling of the enormous black velvet skirts.

The dress had been designed for her by the man she had worked with before she married, Joe Fanucci. An Italian American, he was now far more famous than he had been when Caitlin was one of his top models, and this dress had cost more than she had earned in a year while she had been working for Joe, as she had reminded him, her wide-set blue eyes teasing.

Joe had been amused. 'Yeah, baby,' he had drawled, grinning. 'We both have different price-tags now. The difference is, you can afford me— but I could never afford you!'

She had pretended to laugh, but for her the humour had been slightly bitter. Was that all she was? Was that how the rest of the world saw her? A piece of property with a price-tag?

She finished applying a warm pink gloss to her mouth, and leaned back to survey the result, a tiny frown pleating her brows. Every time she went out in public, she was aware of being watched; by her husband and a host of others. She could never forget whose wife she was; she was expected to look flawless, and sometimes the strain made her want to scream.

'You look beautiful tonight,' said a deep, cool voice from the door, and she sat very still, her eyes flashing to meet the reflection of his in the mirror. She hadn't heard him come into the room; her nerve-ends shrank as if at the touch of fire, but her face stayed calm.

'The dress is an inspiration,' he said slowly, staring. 'You look like a living Renoir.'

That evening they were attending the opening of a comprehensive exhibition of Renoir's paintings, gathered from all over the world, from galleries as far apart as Tokyo, Chicago and Leningrad. Caitlin had ordered the dress from Joe months ago, with this evening in mind. She had learnt to study her engagement diary well in advance, to make sure she had the right clothes for any special occasion. Monro had insisted that she should have a social secretary to guide her and deal with all aspects of her public life, which was some help, but she still felt her life was overcrowded with petty details about which she cared nothing.

'That was the idea!' she said lightly, fighting with the tension of his presence.

'Is it one of your friend Fanucci's dresses?' Monro asked, strolling up behind her. He was wearing elegantly tailored evening clothes, too, but managed to look tough rather than elegant. A tall man, he was physically powerful, with broad shoulders and lean hips, long, athletic legs, all topped by a hard face with piercing grey eyes and an insistent bone structure.

'Yes, Joe made it,' she said, conscious of the grating of his voice as he said Joe's name.

Monro Ritchie was a possessive man; he did not like other men anywhere near her. His jealousy didn't flatter Caitlin; she knew it wasn't personal, merely that what Monro had, he held, against all challengers.

'I don't always like the clothes he makes for you,' he said, frowning. 'I'd rather you went to another designer for a while; it's a mistake only using one house.'

'Very well,' she said without inflection. 'You pay the bills.'

His black brows met. 'You sound angry. Does it matter whether you patronise Fanucci or someone else?'

His grey eyes were steel points of light; he watched her as if waiting for signs of guilt. Surely he didn't suspect her of having an affair with harmless Joe? He must be mad. She shrugged with indifference, the oval mask of her face empty.

'Not in the least. I just happen to like Joe's designs, and he knows what suits me.'

'Well, that he certainly does!' Monro muttered, the flick of his eyes over her body making her prickle. 'But I'd still like you to try someone else for a change.' He slid a hand inside his smooth-fitting jacket and produced a slim, leather-covered box. He flipped the lid back, and she saw the flash of rubies and diamonds in the mirror. 'I saw this in Tiffany's last week while I was in New York. They had to engrave the clasp for me, and it wasn't ready before I left, so they sent it here. What do you think? Do you like it?'

'It's exquisite,' she said, knowing he was going to put the necklace round her throat and tightening up in expectation of his touch.

He leaned forward, the necklace glittering as it swung. Monro's fingertips brushed her bare skin and she shivered.

'Are the stones cold?' he asked drily, his reflected eyes gazing at her reflected breasts where the rubies and diamonds shimmered against pearly skin.

'A little cold,' she said huskily, wishing he would stop staring, stop touching her, because she was intensely uneasy when he looked at her with that darkness in his eyes. She had learnt to recognise the glitter of his desire and to fear it.

'They suit you,' he said, with the touch of sarcasm which he sometimes used. She knew what he implied—he meant that she was cold, too; she and the jewels had that in common, and it was true, but she had warned him. He couldn't deny it. Of course, he hadn't believed her sombre insistence that she didn't love him, couldn't love him, would never again love any man. His male ego wouldn't accept it as true, but she thought he was beginning to believe her now. Was he learning to hate her, too?

He fastened the necklace while she sat in frozen obedience, like a statue, her blue eyes blind in the smooth beauty of her face. Monro Ritchie straightened and stared at her for a long moment, his hands gripping her shoulders, then he bent his head and kissed the naked white, swanlike curve of her neck. His mouth was fierce, angry, almost punitive. He knew she didn't want him to kiss her and he resented it.

Caitlin controlled the shudder that ran through her. She didn't move, scarcely breathed, until Monro lifted his head again and moved away, his face hard and sardonic.

'Well, I suppose we haven't got time for pleasure,' he drawled, and she flushed. 'We mustn't be late!' he added, strolling to the door. He opened it, stood back and waited for her, watching her come towards him.

She walked past him, a white mink jacket around her shoulders, her blonde head held high under that inimical stare, her dress rustling around her, the hem of the long skirt held up by one hand in case she tripped over it. Her face was calm, but she was agitated by the prospect of a twenty-minute drive in the back of the Rolls, alone with Monro.

Their butler was waiting in the hall, Monro's evening cloak and top hat presented with a bow before Austell opened the heavy front door for them and bowed them out. No doubt he much preferred the months when they were out of England at one of Monro's other houses, in Switzerland or Monte Carlo or the Bahamas. For much of the year the English servants had little to do. Monro employed local people when he was in other countries, although he had a head housekeeper, Mrs Tallent, who permanently moved between all his homes, making sure that they were kept in good order, checking on the other staff and hiring new ones if the need arose. Caitlin had been nervous of all those servants at first, but Mrs Tallent had soon put her at her ease.

She had insisted that she was quite happy either to go on running all the domestic details of Monro's life—or to hand over to Caitlin if that was what she wished.

Aghast, Caitlin had said, 'Oh, I couldn't!' imagining herself giving orders to some of the haughty staff she had met so far, and Mrs Tallent had given her a motherly, faintly pitying look.

'My dear Mrs Ritchie, you must not forget that you have one enormous advantage over the staff! You are his wife! Never forget that, and none of them ever will either. However, for the moment, perhaps I had better go on with my job. But, if you'll permit me, I will tutor you in everything I have to do, so that when the day arises you can take over from me without hesitation.

Caitlin had only been twenty-four then; she had badly needed just such support, and so Mrs Tallent went on running the various houses owned by Monro or his companies, with Caitlin as an apprentice, learning all she could, but much happier spending time with Gill, with the kind permission of Mrs Day, who had been Gill's nanny since she was born and had had to be convinced that the new Mrs Ritchie was not going to be a cruel stepmother before she would permit her to take Gill anywhere. Caitlin had learnt diplomacy, among other things, since she had married Monro.

As they came down the steps from the portico, the chauffeur sprang to attention, opening the passenger door of the white Rolls-Royce. Caitlin settled herself well back into the corner, as far away from Monro as she dared without being too obvious about it. He gave her a sideways look, but he said nothing. The Rolls purred down the drive and out of the electronically controlled gates. The house was on the St John's Wood side of Regent's Park. It stood alone, in a large garden, with smooth lawns, immaculate flowerbeds and a line of trees, surrounded by a high stone wall. Both the wall and the ornate iron gates were electronically secure, and at night there were guard dogs loose among the trees.

Monro did not intend anyone to get either into or out of the house without permission. Caitlin often felt like a prisoner in a luxury prison, but after nearly two years of marriage she knew better than to complain to Monro. She was one of his expensive possessions, and, like his other possessions, she was well guarded.

The sound of ringing broke into her thoughts and made her jump. Aware of her start, Monro gave her a nod of formal apology. 'Excuse me, my dear. I think this is an important call I've been expecting.' He leaned forward and unhooked the white and gold car phone. 'Yes?' He listened, his profile enigmatic. Watching him, Caitlin could not guess what sort of news he was being given—good, bad or indifferent. She had been told many times that he was a brilliant poker player, and she believed it. His face could become a blank mask.

'Very well,' he said curtly at last. 'Mexico City, then. Go ahead.'

Caitlin couldn't hide the jolt of shock, and as he hung up Monro met her eyes and frowned.

'What's wrong? Aren't you well? You're very pale.'

'It's nothing,' she stammered, fighting to control the tremor still running over her, and his cool grey eyes narrowed. She looked away, out of the window, at a row of lighted shop windows, conscious of him watching her and praying he wasn't going to talk about it.

'Of course,' he said slowly. 'I'd completely forgotten—Mexico City...the earthquake...'

She didn't answer, her face averted while in her head she saw a swaying chandelier, a ceiling which crazily bulged inward, fall towards her with a rumbling and crashing sound which almost drowned the terrible screaming, the struggles and fights as people tried to get out.

'Stupid of me not to realise . . . you could only have bad memories of the place. I'm sorry to have reminded you,' Monro said, and took her hand. She tensed, rigid from head to foot. 'You're ice-cold!' he said, rubbing her fingers.

'I'm fine,' she said, pulling free. 'Was that the important call you were expecting?'

It was rare for her to show any interest in his business life, and Monro's mouth indented, but he answered.

'Yes. We had two sites in mind for a new factory, either in Mexico or Brazil. I had asked someone to do an in-depth analysis of both places, and then to give me a brief breakdown of his conclusions, so that I could come to a final decision.'

'And that was it on the phone? You listened to his conclusions, then, snap, said go for Mexico?' Caitlin stared at him, her blue eyes very dark in her pale face, her mouth taut. 'Is it a big factory?'

'It will employ thousands.' His voice was cool and unemphatic, but his face was watchful.

'All those people . . .' She turned her head again to stare into the night, wincing as she remembered Mexico City and the poverty she had seen there, driving through the outskirts of what must surely be the most populated city in the world. It had left her dazed, so many people in such desperate need, fighting for the barest existence: bare-footed children with skin like polished gold and dark, sad eyes, women old before their time, men searching without hope for some way out for themselves and their families. And Monro with one phone-call on his way to a party could create thousands of jobs for them. 'Life isn't a very funny joke,' she said, hardly realising that she had said it aloud.

'No, it isn't,' Monro quietly agreed, his eyes fixed on her profile. 'I shall have to go to Mexico City to finalise the arrangements for the building work. Maybe next month. Would you like to come?'

She trembled, her hands tightly clasped in her lap. 'No!' She swallowed, then tried for a lighter tone. 'No, thank you.'

There was a silence, then he said in that low, careful voice, 'You've never talked about him.'

Her head swung, her eyes very blue, very wide. 'What?' she whispered through parched lips.

'It seems significant,' Monro's stare probed her vulnerable face, and she looked down, hiding whatever her eyes held. 'It's eight years since he died in that earthquake. I've known you for nearly three years, yet you've never even mentioned his name, although you must realise I know all about him.'

She laughed humourlessly at that. When Monro had been pursuing her, before she had even agreed to have a date with him, he had ordered his private secretary, George Abbot, to put together a profile of her—along the lines of the detailed analysis he had just had done on Mexico City and the other possible site for a new factory. Monro saw no reason why he shouldn't use his normal business techniques in his private life, if they were useful.

Monro had casually mentioned what he had done, after they were married, and had seemed surprised when she had become blazingly angry and demanded to be given the file so that she could destroy it. He had picked up the phone and told George to bring her a copy of her file, but the information on her had remained in the great central computer which ran everything from his London office. When she had bitterly complained Monro had pointed out that there was an identical file on him, on anyone connected with the company, and that he held no more information on her than the government did. Anyone, he'd said drily, could find out those details about her life.

That might be true, but all the same Caitlin had hated the idea of so much very private information about her being stored away on tapes somewhere. It made her feel helpless, dehumanised, even though on reading the bare facts George had uncovered she had realised that you could not read a human life from facts.

Nothing had been left out, from her birth in a little Welsh village, to the death of her mother when she was seven and the drowning at sea of her sailor father a year later, leaving her in the care of her grandparents. They had died within a few weeks of each other, from pneumonia caught during one of the worst winters of the century, when she was seventeen. She had been working as a typist at a Welsh colliery. A few months later she had married a surveying engineer called Roddy Butler, who had taken her with him to Mexico, where he had begun a new job with a multinational mining firm. They had only been married for six months when an earthquake had destroyed the hotel in which they had been staying. Roddy had been killed. Caitlin had been buried for five days under tons of rubble. She had been brought out alive and miraculously with very few injuries, and had become a celebrity over night. By one of those strange, ironic twists of fate, she had been catapulted into fame as a model solely because of the publicity after her amazing rescue.

She remembered reading the bare, dreary facts collected by George Abbot and feeling almost that they had nothing to do with her. They told one nothing of what she had felt, only what had happened to her, and she had angrily refused to discuss her past with Monro, saying, 'What is any of that to do with you?'

He was watching her intently now, trying to pick up clues from her expression, so she said flatly, 'I don't like dwelling on the past. What happened then was over years ago; what's the point of talking about it?'

'How can it be over when you can't even bring yourself to mention his name?' Monro's voice cracked like a whip, but she wasn't jumping through any hoops for him.

'He's dead!' she muttered, turning away again, and saw that they were just pulling in through the elaborate ironwork gates of Lydgate House.

Their car was in a long line of other limousines queuing to drop passengers at the bottom of the wide stone steps leading up to the eighteenth-century portico of the famous art gallery. 'We're here!' she said, unconsciously relaxing, and Monro gave a curt bark of laughter.

'What a relief for you!' His voice had the sting of sarcasm, but she ignored the tone, leaning forward to watch a plum-coloured Daimler pause, disgorge two passengers and drive on again.

'Isn't that Paul Elliot's car?' she said lightly, watching a thin, distinguished man climbing the steps. 'He's got the Swedish girl with him again. They've been an item for months. I wonder if it is really serious for once?'

'I don't give a damn about Elliot's love-life,' grated Monro as the Rolls drew to a smooth stop. 'Caitlin, isn't it time—— ?'

He had to break off the sentence; their chauffeur had deftly descended and opened her door, and Caitlin gathered up her long full skirts to step down out of the Rolls. The couple ahead of them glanced back; Paul Elliot raised a hand, smiling down at her.

'Well, now, that is what I call inspired dressing,' he drawled, running a comprehensive gaze over her evening gown, and lifting one very thin brow. 'Did you buy it specially for tonight, or...'

'Ordered it in advance,' she said, joining him and his girlfriend, and smiling at the girl. 'Good evening, Ingrid, how are you?'

'From Joe, of course!' Paul said. He was in his late thirties; his face was well known on television from arts programmes and chat shows, and he was also the art critic on a national newspaper and had written a string of books on the Impressionists.

'Yes, from Joe,' she admitted, conscious of Monro appearing at her side, watching them both with hard grey eyes.

'If he's here tonight, I must remember to tell him he's a genius.' Paul gave a faintly wry look at the man beside her. 'Good evening, Monro. I was hoping to have a word with you, too, tonight. I've just heard of something coming on to the market that might interest you. Something unusual for your modern collection.'

'What?' Monro asked curtly, and Paul shook his head at him.

'Keep your voice down! Do you want someone else to snap it up before you can?' He walked on and Monro fell into step with him. Paul lowered his voice, murmuring so softly that Caitlin didn't catch the rest.

She and Ingrid followed the men, talking about that day's financial news, a sudden change in the bank rate and a probable change in tomorrow's stock markets. Ingrid was a financial analyst, a very serious girl with several degrees to her name, although it was her sexy figure and lovely face that made every man turn to stare as he went past her. Ingrid seemed oblivious of all that male interest. She took money very earnestly indeed.

'What made you go in for studying the money market, Ingrid?' asked Caitlin casually, drifting behind the two men and watching as they reached the portico to be greeted by Nicole Barrett, the wife of the man who had organised this exhibition of Renoir's paintings.

'My father is a banker,' said Ingrid simply.

'In Sweden?'

'Oh, yes, in Stockholm. My family has been in banking for three generations, and my brothers are all in the family business, but I am the first girl to want to work in the financial sector and my father was not very happy at first. I have had to prove myself outside Sweden, but when I go back it will be as a director of the family bank.'

'Well done! You deserve it,' said Caitlin, half her mind on what her husband was saying to Nicole Barrett.

'You're looking very elegant tonight; only a Frenchwoman knows how to wear chic clothes with that instinctive flair!' he was murmuring softly, and Nicole purred, her eyes very bright.

'*Mon cher*, I love you! Why don't you teach my husband how to talk to a woman? After ten years of marriage to me he still has no idea!'

'He's an idiot!'

Nicole had been born in Paris and it showed; she was a very smart, sophisticated woman of thirty-five, with raven-black hair worn in the latest fashion, and dramatic black eyes. Her deep purple dress had a sombre magnificence. Not everyone could wear it, but on Nicole it was stunning. She knew what suited her and what would catch the eye, and although her husband, Jeffrey, was a very wealthy man, her thrifty French training had made her careful always to buy clothes that would last for years and do for any number of different occasions. Caitlin had noticed Nicole's exquisite clothes reappearing over and over again during the two years she had known her.

Caitlin had never actually liked Nicole; they were too different in type. They really had nothing in common, and were only thrown together because their husbands shared an obsession with art and artists.

Tonight, though, Caitlin discovered another reason for not liking Nicole. As she watched the other woman talking to Monro, it slowly dawned on Caitlin that Nicole found him very attractive, and didn't bother to hide it.

Look at her fluttering her false eyelashes at him! Caitlin thought, her brows together. She's flirting shamelessly, and Monro obviously isn't giving her any red light. How long has it been going on? And why did I never notice it before?

Ingrid was talking next to her, but Caitlin didn't hear a word she said. She was remembering the night Monro had proposed to her, two and a half years ago. He had frankly told her that he had had many love-affairs in the past, but, he had promised, there would never be another one after they were married.

For the first time she wondered if he had kept that promise—the idea had never occurred to her before, and if Monro was unfaithful to her she

couldn't in all honesty blame him, but somehow
it disturbed her to think of him having affairs in
secret, especially with the wives of men she knew,
women she met as often as she met Nicole
Barrett.

'Here is your guide,' Ingrid said, handing her
a glossy catalogue of the exhibition's canvases,
with lengthy mention of their provenance. 'I love
Renoir, don't you? He painted real women, and
he painted them with love, not like Picasso, who
painted them with hatred and made them ugly.'

Holding the catalogue, Caitlin followed her
around the first large room, pausing before each
canvas. Ingrid commented with blunt frankness
on each one and Caitlin listened, but her mind
was elsewhere. She was puzzling over her own
reactions to watching Monro with Nicole.

She couldn't be jealous, because she didn't love
him. She never had, she should never have
married him, but Monro hadn't accepted her rejection. He was a stubborn, persistent, tenacious
man who had never yet failed to get what he
wanted, and he had not been able to believe that
he wouldn't get her in the end. She had refused
to see him, but he had finally cornered her at a
party given by Joe Fanucci to which Monro had
wangled an invitation.

Actually, she had been surprised to find him
a pleasant companion. He had stayed at her side
all evening. He had asked her endless questions:
what books she read, what films she saw, how
she felt about politics. Everyone enjoyed talking
about themselves; the evening had flown by. She

had confessed to a love of the theatre, he had
asked if she had seen that year's smash West End
hit, and she had wryly said not yet. You had to
book a year in advance, unless you paid black-
market prices. Monro had laughed and changed
the subject, then the next day he had rung her
up to ask her to see the play with him. He had
got hold of a box. She could only guess at the
price!

That immediate, determined move had alarmed
her for the first time. She had begun to take
Monro's pursuit seriously, and to feel nervous of
him. Of course, she should have refused to go to
the play, but she hadn't, because she'd really
wanted to see it.

Elated by a wonderful performance of the play,
she had gone on to supper afterwards with him
at the Café Royal, where Oscar Wilde and
Bernard Shaw and so many of the literary and
theatrical giants of turn-of-the-century London
had gathered to talk. The red plush and chan-
deliers still had a feel of that period, and famous
people still, apparently, ate there. One of them
had been a writer she had admired for a long
time. Monro had introduced her to him, and she
had been very excited by their brief talk.

He had asked her to a party. At once Monro
had said that he would bring her. That had been
another moment when she should have refused;
she'd been riding an express train into marriage
with him, but she hadn't realised it then. It had
all happened so fast, and apparently so naturally; it had been an unstoppable process.

Monro had meant to have her in spite of her angry, blunt declaration that she didn't love him, couldn't love him. He had pushed that aside. It didn't matter, he had said, then. But it did, of course; she increasingly felt that it did. Monro was bitter because she gave him nothing but her body, and he less and less seemed to want that. It almost seemed to make him angry to make love to her, even though she never refused to sleep with him. She had made a bargain, and she kept her side, but was Monro happy with his side of the bargain?

She should never have agreed to the marriage, but once she had met Gill she had been trapped. Gill had touched the heart Caitlin had thought dead. She had been so small and lonely in that enormous house; she had only been four the first time they had met. Monro hadn't let Caitlin glimpse his child until after her first rejection of him.

He had never talked about his first marriage— any more than she had talked to him about hers. She hadn't realised for some time that he had a child, then she'd realised that he was afraid she might be put off by the discovery, might resent or be jealous of her. Once he'd seen that Caitlin loved children and was enchanted by Gill, he'd made certain that Caitlin saw her as often as possible, and that was typical of him, to seize every opportunity he saw, to use her own nature against her. He was a clever man with a complex mind, and he could be devious to get what he wanted.

She had often wondered why he wanted her so badly. She rapidly realised that there were plenty of much lovelier women around who wanted him and made no secret of it—but then wasn't that human nature? To want what was out of reach, but not to want what was easy to get?

Monro had been determined to marry her, and when she'd refused he'd tackled that the way he solved his business problems—he'd coolly looked for a way to make her change her mind, and found it. Instead of asking her to be his wife, he'd asked her to become Gill's mother.

Gill had desperately wanted a mother because her father was so busy and she had no family life at all. She had spent her life with her nanny, of whom she was fond, but she had innocently blurted out more than once how much she had longed to have a mummy of her own, like other children. Caitlin had seen in Gill something of herself, of course; the death of her own parents when she was small had left her very lonely. Gill had touched her deeply from the beginning, but it had been more than that. Caitlin had known she couldn't bear to fall in love with a man again, but it had seemed safe to love a child who needed her. Caitlin had finally said yes to Monro, but only after he had said he accepted that she did not love him, it didn't matter, he was sure they could still make a good life together.

It had been a dangerous, stupid bargain to make—she should have known it was bound to go wrong. But a coldness settled around her heart as she wondered what she would do if Monro was tired of their loveless marriage and wanted a divorce.

Ingrid was chattering next to her as they walked through the exhibition, but Caitlin didn't hear a word. She stared at Renoir's canvases and wasn't really seeing them. She was aware of Monro some way behind them, with Nicole Barrett. Nicole had a hand on his dark-sleeved arm; he was watching her sideways with a smile Caitlin recognised—a mocking curve of the mouth which held sensuality, too, an amused sexual awareness. He had often looked at Caitlin like that. She had never responded the way Nicole was doing—the other woman was staring back at him and smiling in the same way, her hand was pressing down on his arm, her hip was touching his.

My God! They're practically making love in public, right before my very eyes! thought Caitlin, with a burning indignation which was growing like a forest fire raging through dry wood. She had never liked Nicole, who was a man's woman and disliked and despised her own sex.

She wasn't jealous, she assured herself. She didn't love Monro—why should she be jealous? But what if Monro did divorce her?

She would lose Gill. Gill was Monro's child, not hers, and she would never be given custody in a divorce case. Monro wouldn't consider giving her custody, either. He did love Gill, even if he was often too busy to see much of her.

He might let Caitlin visit Gill from time to time, but he would not let Gill live with her, and

Caitlin loved her. Gill was the only human being in the world she had loved since that day in Mexico City when the sky had fallen in on her.

'Ah, this is the buffet-room...now we get champagne, I think,' said Ingrid with satisfaction as they walked into a final room where Jeffrey Barrett was welcoming guests. A stocky, burly man with a slightly balding head, he was a good ten years older than his wife, whom he seemed to regard with proprietorial pride rather than love.

'White wine, I'm afraid,' said Jeffrey Barrett, greeting them and lifting two glasses from a tray held by a waiter. 'We couldn't afford champagne. Hello, Ingrid, you gorgeous little Swede! Don't I get a kiss? Mmm...thanks! And one from you, Caitlin, darling? Where's your husband? Didn't he come with you?'

She was clutching the stem of her wine glass and staring blankly, not really hearing him.

'Oh, there he is,' Jeffrey said, his smile twisting. 'Flirting with my wife again! You ought to put your foot down, Caitlin. You shouldn't let him get away with it.'

She was frozen on the spot, her skin icy cold. Around her people talked and laughed, but Caitlin was in a state of bitter shock, struggling to think, to understand what was happening. It couldn't be true. She was going mad, she had to be; it couldn't be true.

The waiter was watching her; he had seen her white face, the trembling of the hand gripping the wine glass. He hurriedly removed the glass from her clenched fingers just as Monro and Nicole sauntered up to join the little group around Caitlin.

As if the waiter's thoughtful action had pressed a trigger, Caitlin toppled forward in a dead faint.

CHAPTER TWO

THE black-out was complete. When Caitlin recovered consciousness, for a few seconds she remembered nothing, and as her lashes fluttered, sensing the presence of light, her first impression was that she must be waking up in bed in the morning, until she heard voices and was bewildered.

'This way, Monro, bring her in here! Put her down on the sofa.'

'No,' contradicted a voice she recognised as that of Jeffrey Barrett. 'Put her on the chair, and push her head down, between her knees. You have to bring the blood back into her head.'

She was being carried by someone, her head against his shoulder, her body supported with apparent ease by one of his arms under her back, the other under her knees. She didn't feel afraid he would drop her, but her heart began to beat faster and she breathed roughly.

'Here . . .' one of the voices said, and Monro lowered her carefully until she was sitting on a chair, then she felt his hand on the nape of her neck, forcing her head downwards. She didn't struggle; she needed time to think about what had made her faint. She bowed under his hand, her body limp, let her head hang and felt the strange icy coldness dissolving slowly and her mind clearing, then the memory strengthened and darkened and she began to tremble convulsively.

'I'm a doctor,' said a strange voice from a distance. 'Can I help?'

'That's very good of you. Yes, my wife just fainted, and she doesn't seem at all well.'

'She might feel rather better if you allowed her to sit up. No doubt she is feeling dizzy with her head down there.' The strange voice was ironic and much closer.

Monro slid an arm around her shoulders and carefully lifted her into an upright position again. She kept her eyes shut and fought to control the trembling. Nobody must guess. That was vital. Nobody must guess.

She didn't know what to do. She only knew she had to get away from here. She had to be alone to think, to work out what to do, to understand what it meant...

'I can't examine a patient in a room full of people,' said the doctor's dry voice. 'Mr Ritchie, if you would stay, please—and if the rest of you would please leave us?'

'Of course,' said Jeffrey. 'If there's anything you need, just ask for it, Monro. I'll be right outside, if you need me.'

'Thanks, Jeffrey.'

A door closed and the room became very quiet; so quiet that she could hear herself breathing.

'Firstly, let's ask the obvious,' the doctor said with a smile in his voice. 'Is your wife pregnant, Mr Ritchie?'

There was a silence, then Monro said slowly, 'Not to my knowledge.'

There was another pause. They were watching her. She felt them staring, then Monro asked flatly, 'Are you, Caitlin?'

That was when she had to open her eyes. She did not look at Monro. She looked at the doctor; he was a middle-aged man with greying hair and a pleasant face. She shook her head, afraid to risk speaking in case her voice no longer worked. He smiled at her.

'Sure about that?'

She nodded, still scared to open her mouth.

'Well, then, having eliminated that possibility, let's make a few checks, shall we?' He put cold fingers on her wrist, listening to her pulse. She watched him, and felt Monro watching her. His grey eyes probed her defences, but she had had time now to make her mind impregnable to him. She knew her expression wouldn't betray what had happened to her a few moments ago.

The doctor relinquished her wrist, that professional smile even brighter. 'Nothing worrying there. Any headache? Dizziness? Or nausea?'

She shook her head. 'I think I fainted because there were far too many people in there, the oxygen was running out.' She tried a weak smile and he smiled back. 'And I'd been on my feet for ages. The wine probably didn't help, either.'

'So that's your theory, is it?' He smiled in a paternal way. 'Well, not a bad one, at that. People are always fainting in stuffy, over-crowded rooms. How do you feel now?'

'Better.'

He studied her pallor, perhaps read the tension in her body, the way her hands tightly gripped the chair arms, the drawn look of her mouth.

'Perhaps all you need is a good night's sleep?'

'Probably,' she said, trying to laugh.

'Then I should go home at once, and get to bed,' he said. 'If you have any further trouble, call your own doctor at once, Mrs Ritchie. A faint can be a symptom of any number of diseases, or it can be something very minor, but it should never just be ignored.'

She nodded, forcing a smile. The doctor left and Monro sat on a velvet-covered stool close beside her and stared, frowning.

'I never remember you fainting before.'

'I don't think I ever have,' she said irritably, evading the searching grey eyes. 'Can we go home?'

Home! she thought, her stomach sinking as if she were in a lift which was out of control, tumbling down floor by floor at terrible speed. She had a sense of panic. Home! How much longer would it be that to her? Her head was crowding with realisations of the consequences of tonight. Her life was in ruins. She couldn't bear the glimpses of the future which kept coming to her.

Monro was still frowning. 'I wish I knew what was wrong. Something is, I'm sure about that— why won't you tell me?'

'I'm just so tired!' She yawned, quite naturally; fear and shock were sapping her energy, making her tired, making her yawn.

'Yes, of course, I'm sorry,' Monro said at once, looking concerned. 'I'll carry you.'

'There's no need!' She stumbled to her feet, swaying slightly, and Monro made an exasperated sound, like a growl, his arm going round her waist. 'I can walk,' she said huskily. 'I'm much too heavy for you to carry me all the way out to the car, and I don't want people staring.'

She thought of walking back through the room where she had fainted, where the waiters would still be circulating with wine, and the other guests still standing about exchanging the usual gossip, no doubt speculating as to why she had fainted. She had only been married two years, and hadn't had a child yet. Like the doctor, that was the first possibility that would spring to their minds. She could not bear to walk through those rooms with those eyes watching her all the way.

'Is there another way out?' she asked with faint desperation.

'I'll ask Jeffrey,' Monro said, opening the door without letting go of her waist.

Jeffrey was standing guard, right outside the door, and when Monro explained he at once said, 'Of course, I'll show you the back way out, but what about your car? Look, wait here—I'll arrange for your chauffeur to drive round to the back and pick you up there. I'll be back as soon as I've found him.'

Caitlin sat down again, leaned back and shut her eyes. At once her mind began working. How was she going to find out if she hadn't imagined it? She had to know for sure. She couldn't rest until she knew.

A private detective? That was so shabby! She hated the idea of using such methods. Yet how else could she discover the truth?

'Caitlin...' Monro said huskily.

She had to open her eyes. 'Yes?' She gave him a glance which hurriedly sheered away. It hurt to look at him. He seemed remote suddenly, unfamiliar to her; there was uncertainty in his grey eyes. She saw a nervous little tic beating next to his mouth.

'Are you sure you couldn't be pregnant?' His voice had a rough edge. Did he want her to be pregnant? They had never talked about having children, and she had been taking precautions all along. It wasn't so much that she did not want a baby as that she had had no idea how Monro felt, but he must have known that she was taking care not to get pregnant, so he couldn't have wanted a child.

'Sure!' she said, her mouth twisting. It was just as well. If she had had a baby, Monro would probably have fought to keep it when they separated, and she was in no psychological state to face a bitter fight over a child. Everything was complicated and painful enough without that.

A silence fell, then the door opened and Jeffrey was back. 'OK, I spoke to your man. He's driving round there now. By the time we make our way through the maze of corridors that were the servants' quarters here, your car should be waiting right outside the back entrance.'

'Thanks, Jeffrey, this is very good of you,' Monro said, as they followed him through the narrow and badly lit corridors.

'Not at all. I hope Caitlin is better tomorrow. It was very hot in there. Far too many people, but it seems to have gone off well.'

'It's the best exhibition I've seen for years,' Monro congratulated him. 'Wonderful to see so many Renoirs all at once, and fascinating to follow the development through the years—something you never get a chance to do normally, seeing a painting in a museum in London, then some in France, then a couple in the States. You don't get a clear idea of the artist's growth of technique from seeing pictures out of context.'

'No, quite,' said Jeffrey in a soulful voice. 'Precisely my reason for setting up the exhibition in the first place. And it has been an excellent turn-out, especially as there was a gala performance at Covent Garden tonight, and a lot of important people had to be there. That was practically the sole reason for most of the rejections we had, in fact. If they could have been here, they would have been. I just knew it was time for another Renoir exhibition. Everyone knows the famous paintings, but he left so much stuff that hasn't been over-popularised. Well, we're setting it right now. Ah, here we are...now, what did I do with that key? Oh, yes, my waistcoat pocket.'

Jeffrey stopped talking to unlock the door, which he threw open. Caitlin took a deep breath of cool, fresh air as she emerged into the night.

The chauffeur was waiting, as promised; he opened the passenger door and Monro took her arm to slide her inside the limousine.

'Thank you, Jeffrey. Goodnight,' said Monro, getting in beside her, then the chauffeur closed the door after him and walked round to get behind the wheel. Jeffrey bent to wave at them, and the car began to move slowly away. Monro raised a casual hand in farewell to Jeffrey, then they were out of sight and Caitlin could lean back into the corner of the seat, her eyes fixed on the sky she could just see between London roofs. Tonight, the moon was filmed with light drifts of gauzy cloud, and there weren't many stars. She stared at them and wished she were on one of them, light years away from here.

There was little traffic around now. Before she expected it, they were home, and as they entered the house she heard the long case clock in the hall chiming eleven. Was it so early? She felt as if she had been away for hours. It had only been a short time after all; yet her whole life had been turned upside-down and would never be the same again.

She got little sleep that night. Monro did not come to her room, but that was not unusual now. He more and more often slept alone in his own suite of rooms, on the other side of the corridor. When they were first married, he had made love to her frequently, often several times a night, and would go to sleep with her held in his arms, their bodies fitting together as if they were made for each other. The very memory of his passion made her twist restlessly in her bed. He hadn't made love to her like that for a long time. After two years of marriage, his desire for her had obviously been sated, she thought bitterly. He would probably be relieved when he found out that their marriage was over. She would be saving him the problem of asking her for a divorce; he ought to be grateful!

Monro left for his office every morning at an unearthly hour, long before she was usually awake, so she did not expect to see him when she got up. She always had her breakfast in bed, brought in by her maid, a woman of fifty whose job was mainly to look after Caitlin's large wardrobe. Julie spent her days washing, ironing, pressing, mending. She had once been a theatrical dresser, and still talked nostalgically about life backstage, but she could no longer stay up late every night. She worked from eight until four, for Caitlin, and those hours suited her much better than theatrical hours did.

Caitlin had dropped into a light doze from sheer exhaustion around dawn, but she woke up at once when the door of her bedroom opened. She heard the rattle of the tray as Julie crossed the room, and opened her eyes reluctantly, wincing at the stab of morning light as Julie opened the curtains with a touch of an electronic button.

Caitlin sat up, pushed her pillows to give her more support, and gave Julie a smile.

But it wasn't Julie; it was Monro in a dark pin-striped suit, his lean face cleanly shaven, his hair faintly damp from his shower.

'How are you this morning? I brought your breakfast myself, so that I could see how you were before I left for the office.' He gave her one of his charming smiles, his grey eyes wandering over her bare, pale shoulders, the warmly clinging white silk nightdress which covered but did not hide her rounded breasts. Monro's eyes came back to her face, and he frowned.

'You still don't look well. Didn't you sleep? Maybe you're hatching something nasty. I'll get Austell to ring the doctor. You had better stay in bed until he gets here, and, if he says you're ill, stay there until he says you can get up.'

He bent to place her tray across her lap as Caitlin protested. 'I'm fine, there's no need for a doctor. I have lots to do today, I can't stay in bed.'

'I want you to see the doctor,' Monro insisted. 'Are you going to eat your breakfast?'

'Of course!' she said, pretending eagerness as she sipped some of the freshly squeezed orange juice, served very chilled, in a glass held by a silver goblet. She poured herself a cup of coffee from the silver pot, nibbled one of the crisp, flaky croissants made that morning by Monro's French chef.

Monro watched her for a moment, then bent and kissed her lightly on the cheek. She tensed as he came closer, her whole body rigid. She knew she would never be able to bear Monro to touch her again.

He gave her a narrow-eyed stare as he straightened. She sensed that he had picked up her tension, but his voice remained calm.

'Don't forget—stay in bed until the doctor arrives! I'll ring you later, between meetings.'

'There's no need to do that!'

'I want to know what the doctor says.' He walked to the door, paused there to look back. She pretended to be eating, her head lowered. The door closed and she sagged, giving a long, painful sigh.

She couldn't bear much more of this tension. It was so hard not to blurt out what was in her mind, but she knew she mustn't say a word yet. First she had to be certain she hadn't imagined it. She had to get hold of a detective at once and have an investigation made. It couldn't be difficult; there must be an easy trail to follow.

She drank some strong black coffee, ignoring the croissants now that Monro wasn't there to see her, then she slid out of bed and hurried to the bathroom to shower, and back to her bedroom to get dressed. She was in bra and panties when the phone rang, and she picked up the receiver without any premonition in her mind.

'Yes?' Her mind was working on the problem of how to get in touch with a private detective, how to pay him, without Monro finding out.

'Madam, I have Mr Barrett on the phone. Do you want to speak to him?' asked Austell, the butler, in his most neutral of voices, and she grimaced faintly. She was in no mood to talk to Jeffrey. She could guess why he had rung her— to find out what was behind that faint! But he would keep ringing if she didn't talk to him, so she shrugged.

'Put him on, please, Austell.'

'Thank you, Madam.'

A click and then a voice; but not Jeffrey's voice, although it sounded very similar.

'Caitlin?'

Her hand tightened on the telephone; she turned white and was too shocked to make a sound.

'Caitlin,' he said again, very softly. 'We have a lot to talk about. Meet me in the Food Hall at Harrods at eleven o'clock sharp.'

'I can't——' she got out before the phone went dead. She sat down abruptly on the bed. What was she going to do?

She had to go. She had no choice. He knew that. She stared at the little Indian clock beside her bed; carved ivory and gold, it was a marvellous and lovely thing, and it ticked almost silently. Nine o'clock. She had plenty of time before the deadline, time to make up her mind what to do. But her mind was made up already. She knew she was going to go.

Why had she thought she would have to track him down with private detectives? She should have known better. She hadn't needed to look for him. He had found her. Only then did she start to wonder...had he found her before last night? Had he been at that reception to make sure she saw him? But if he had known how to find her why hadn't he been in touch before this morning? Was he playing games with her?

What's he up to? she wondered, remembering all she knew about him, the bad dreams she had spent years trying to forget. Last night she had thought it was pure accident, that glimpse of each other—but now in the cold light of day she knew it was not chance that had brought them together again. He had intended that meeting. He had plans for her.

She dressed slowly because her hands were shaking, then she went out on to the landing to lean over the banister and listen. She didn't want to run into Austell or any other member of staff. No doubt Monro had given them instructions to make sure she didn't go out.

The hall was empty; she ran downstairs, hardly making a sound, and was out of the front door within seconds. She took a taxi to Hyde Park first and walked under the trees for half an hour, trying to work out what she should do, but she could only speculate about the reasons behind this summons, so eventually she took another taxi to Kensington, to Harrods.

She had a leisurely coffee there, just to pass the time, sitting at a table in a corner, with the cup in front of her, staring into blank space, remembering, dreading the moment when she had to meet him.

Just before eleven o'clock she walked slowly down the marble stairs to the ground floor, to the great Food Hall which was one of the most famous sights of London. It was always crowded with people: sightseers, tourists, men wistfully hunting for their wives who had come in there an hour ago and never re-emerged, children hungrily staring at rich and indigestible cakes, housewives looking for something different for dinner, at the fish stall, with its marble counter draped with fishing nets and an incredible array of fish, or hesitating between duck and venison on the game counter, or trying to decide whether their guests would prefer Red Leicester cheese or Camembert at the cheese counter. You could buy anything edible in the world there; fabulous delicacies crowded together under the famous roof through which a pale light filtered, showing Caitlin the sea of strange faces moving in an endless stream around the various counters, in and out of the entrances on all sides of the hall.

How was she going to find him in this crowd? Somebody pushed her from behind and she started, looking round. A large lady in a flowered hat said impatiently, 'Excuse me!'

'Oh, sorry,' Caitlin stammered, letting her pass, only to find someone else trying to get round her. You could not stand still in the Food Hall of Harrods or you would get trampled underfoot.

She began to make her way around the great room, constantly looking at faces but not recognising any of them.

Suddenly she saw him and stopped dead, staring. He looked very different this morning. He wasn't dressed as a waiter now in formal dark clothes. He was wearing shabby jeans, trainers on his feet, an old army sweater, olive-green, with leather on the shoulders, at the elbows. He hadn't shaved and his face was rough with golden stubble, but that only made him look sexier, and Caitlin was far from being the only woman staring at him. Other female eyes glanced, did a double-take and widened with sexual interest. His corn-blond hair was cut very short, close to his head; his very light blue eyes had a brilliance which was a threat. His slim, boyish figure and that finely chiselled face might have been effeminate if it weren't for the personality of the man himself. He was no boy. He was past thirty, he had an animal magnetism, and knew it, lounging there arrogantly, staring back at Caitlin with a mocking little smile curling his lips.

She looked at him with fear and hatred, and the smile curved deeper lines around his mouth. He was pleased with her expression, and she gritted her teeth. She must try to hide her feelings. It was dangerous to betray anything to him. He was expert at hunting for vulnerable places; he was an emotional terrorist, looking for a soft target.

He turned away, walking slowly, and she followed, as he had known she would, because she had no choice. Where was he leading her? They came out into the street and he hailed a taxi which had just dropped a fare.

He stood back and waved Caitlin into the back of the cab, told the driver, 'Kensington Gardens!'

and got in beside her. She shifted away, along the seat, staring out of the window.

The taxi moved off and the man beside her lounged back, his jean-clad legs stretched out in assured relaxation. He watched her tense profile, but he didn't say anything, and the silence ate at her nerves.

When he did speak she jumped, in spite of her determination to keep cool.

'So,' was all he said, slowly, and then she jumped and he laughed softly. 'You ought to see a doctor about those nerves!'

She bit down on her inner lip and ignored him. It was the only defence she had for the moment: silence.

'I must say,' he drawled, 'I never thought you'd turn out to be quite such a beauty! You were a pretty kid, of course, but a little insipid. Alice in Wonderland, with a hairband and long blonde curls, hardly any make-up, big blue eyes and a demure expression. No, you didn't set the world on fire in those days, but I can see you've learnt a lot since then.'

She didn't look at him, but she knew he was smiling, she heard it in his voice, and a shudder ran down her back. His smiles were lethal. What was he planning? If only she knew what to expect! She was icy cold and she felt sick. She couldn't believe it, though. She simply could not believe that she was sitting here in a London taxi with him. It was a living nightmare. If only she could wake up and find that that was all it was . . . just a nightmare, not real at all.

'Who taught you?' he murmured in that soft voice which wouldn't reach the ears of the taxi-driver, safely behind his glass shield. 'How many men have there been since I had you, Caitlin? Quite a few, I should imagine. I'm going to enjoy finding out just how much you've learnt.'

Nausea rose in her throat. She turned on him, then, tormented beyond endurance, her loathing in her face, her voice shaking. 'You . . . I'd rather die than have you lay a finger on me! I'd kill you if you tried.'

The taxi stopped suddenly at traffic lights, and she was flung sideways, toppling on to his knees. He caught her, one hand carelessly, cruelly, twisting into her hair and holding her down across his lap as she began to struggle up.

The taxi moved on again; he shot a glance at the driver's back, as if to make sure the man wasn't watching them, then his head came down while Caitlin writhed and fought to escape. He tightened his grip on her hair and she gave a muffled cry of pain, then his mouth was crushing down on her parted lips. It wasn't so much a kiss as an assault, without mercy, hurting and enjoying the pain he was inflicting.

She brought her teeth together in his lip and he gave an angry exclamation. He sat up, scowling, fingering his lower lip where the flesh was torn and blood trickled.

'You vicious little bitch! You'll pay for that!'

The taxi stopped again, and this time it was because they had reached their destination.

'Kensington Gardens—this entrance OK?' asked the driver, turning to face them.

'Fine,' the man beside her said, his face averted
so that the driver shouldn't notice his bitten lip.
He got out of the taxi and paid the driver while
she was getting out. She slowly walked into the
gardens while the taxi was driving away. The
lawns were immaculately kept, as smooth as the
baize on a billiard-table, with pools of bluish
shadow spreading around the trees. A warm,
honeyed fragrance drifted from the roses, birds
sang among the branches of beech and lime-tree,
bees drowsily hummed from one blossom to another, and children ran between the benches
placed here and there, playing, arguing, laughing,
while their mothers watched them and chattered
to each other about the price of fish and the latest
fashions for toddlers.

It was a peaceful, familiar scene on a summer's day in England—and the atmosphere was
wildly at odds with the violence inside Caitlin,
the anger and the fear of the man catching up
with her now.

'Let's walk,' he said, and he had himself in
control again. He was even smiling, but it was
not a pleasant smile.

They walked, and Caitlin waited for him to
come out with whatever he meant to do to her.
He had the upper hand, he held all the cards. She
had so much to lose; she was utterly at his mercy,
and she knew him well enough to know he would
have no mercy. He was a ruthless man who would
destroy her life just to amuse himself.

They turned into a less frequented path under
trees and he gestured to a bench. 'Let's sit here.'

She obeyed, her hands clasped in her lap to stop them trembling, her head bent as she waited for the blow.

He turned towards her, one arm along the green wooden back of the bench. The scent of roses was stifling, sickening.

'I like your earrings,' he drawled. 'Sapphires suit you, they bring out the blue of your eyes.' He reached out a hand and almost wrenched one of the earrings from her. 'Sorry, did that hurt?' he murmured mockingly. 'Oh, what a pity...your earlobe is bleeding...'

'You did that deliberately!' she muttered, rubbing her ear and seeing the trace of blood on her fingers.

'Tit for tat,' he agreed, running the tip of his tongue along his lower lip where she had bitten it. He held out his hand. 'Give me the other earring.'

Silently she took it off and gave it to him. He held both delicate jewels in his palm, weighing them and staring down at them.

'What are they worth? A thousand?' It was an accurate guess, but she didn't answer. He smiled. 'Yes, around that. Well, I'll keep them on account. I'm sure you won't miss these trinkets, and I need money in a hurry. I owe someone rather a large amount, and if I don't come up with it by Friday I shall be in bad trouble. If I sell these, what I get for them will keep my creditor quiet until you get the rest of the money to me.'

'How much?' she asked, for a moment almost relieved to realise that it was money he was after. Yet if she paid, would he go away? Her common sense warned her—of course he wouldn't! He would milk her for every penny he could get; he would still destroy her marriage, but it would take longer. It would happen little by little, death by a thousand cuts instead of sudden death. Which would be worse?

'Only twenty thousand,' he said coolly, and she gasped.

'Twenty thousand pounds? I haven't got that sort of money!'

'The wife of one of the richest men in the country? Of course you have. That must be pocket money to you! Why, the necklace you were wearing last night was worth far more than twenty thousand!'

'That was a present from my husband——'

'Your what?' he asked, eyes insolent, and she drew an agonised breath, staring back at him. 'I am your husband, Caitlin.'

CHAPTER THREE

'No,' CAITLIN muttered in sick revulsion, shaking her head.

'Legally, I am,' he drawled. 'And that's all that matters. You committed bigamy, Caitlin, sweetie, and you could go to prison for that. I can see the newspapers now...they'd have a field day. Billionaire and wife in court on bigamy charge—do they charge both parties? Or is it just the bigamous one who goes to jail? I suppose it wouldn't be fair on the other one—if he didn't know it was bigamy, that is! Have you told him I'm alive yet?' He shot her a sideways look.

'No, I was too shocked last night,' she whispered. 'I thought I might have imagined I'd seen you. What were you doing there, working as a waiter?'

'I just got back to England from Australia, and I needed money while I was looking for a job, so I took on this temporary job as a waiter.'

She looked bitterly at him. 'You haven't changed, have you?'

'Neither, I'm glad to see, have you,' he mocked, his eyes spiteful. 'I recognised you at once as I was holding that tray. You could have knocked me down with a feather, especially when I found out you had married again—and who you had married! You wouldn't like prison, darling, not after your luxurious life with Monro Ritchie... what an apt name he has, too! I did a little checking up on him since I saw you last night. He must be so rich he doesn't even know himself how much he has tucked away. That doesn't seem fair, does it? That he should have all that money—and my wife, too!'

'I thought you were dead!'

'Well, you would say that, wouldn't you?' He merely smiled.

'The Mexican authorities thought so too! You were legally declared dead, burnt to death in the fire that destroyed half that hotel after the earthquake. If I'd stayed in the bar with you that night, I might have died, too. That was what saved my life—the fact that I'd gone to bed early.'

'OK, OK, I didn't ask you to relive it!' Roddy said impatiently, but she just went on in a deadly quiet voice, as if he weren't there, as if she were a record he had put on, but could not turn off.

'I was asleep when the first tremor began. I woke up falling with the bed, it was pitch-black, and there was crashing and screaming all around me. I didn't understand what was happening; I screamed, too, then I lost consciousness, and when I woke up I couldn't see anything. I was buried in the rubble. It was terrifying to lie there, unable to move, unable to see, hearing people crying and groaning. I tried to call out, but nobody heard me... I was trapped under a beam that had fallen through the ceiling above—that was what kept me alive, they said later; somehow I was in a pocket of air and cushioned by my own bed, but the beam kept most of the rubble from crushing me. It took the rescue services days to dig down to where I was, and all that time I thought I was going to die.'

'Yes, I read about it,' he said coolly. 'Quite the little heroine! Pages of pictures and descriptions of your terrifying experience, the miracle of finding you alive and almost unharmed.' His twisted smile was a sneer. 'Fascinating reading.'

'You read about it?' She turned her head to stare at him. 'But that means you must have known that I thought you were dead—that was in the papers too, that I had only been married for a few months and my husband had died in the fire that started in the bar.'

'That was what gave me the idea; reading my own obituary. As Mark Twain said, when it happened to him, "The report of my death was an exaggeration."' He laughed, but Caitlin didn't even smile. She saw nothing remotely funny in what he was saying. Roddy shrugged his indifference to her lack of amusement. 'Well, as the world had decided I was dead, I didn't see why I should disillusion them. I stayed dead.'

'But . . . why?' she asked hoarsely, and Roddy grimaced, smoothing down his hair with one hand, which, she noted with disbelief, was totally steady. She might be as jumpy as a cat, but he wasn't.

'I hate to say this, sweetie, but I wanted to get away from you. I was bored with you. I'd been planning to walk out for quite a while.' He gave her a charming smile, as though inviting her to enjoy the joke. 'That quake was a positive godsend!'

'You bastard!' she burst out, and a young man in a white tracksuit who was jogging past them at that moment turned his head in curious surprise to stare. Caitlin waited until he was a few yards further on before she hissed at Roddy, 'I'm no bigamist. You just admitted that you meant everyone to think you were dead. I didn't know you weren't.'

'I'd tell everyone you did,' he threatened calmly, and she looked at him in utter incredulity. He smiled, 'I would tell them that we cooked it up between us, for the insurance money. I played dead and you collected the insurance money, then we were supposed to meet up again somewhere else, and share it.'

'But I didn't get any insurance money! The insurance company refused to pay me because I couldn't produce a body! They said I would have to wait three years before they would pronounce you dead.'

'Really?' He looked genuinely surprised at that. 'Well, well, the cheapskates! I had no idea. Sorry about that. I did mean you to get that money, you know.'

'It wasn't much,' she muttered grimly.

He shrugged. 'The policy was all I could afford, but I thought it would pay your fare back to England and give you a fresh start somewhere. You might give me credit for good intentions. You had been one of my bigger mistakes. I should never have married you, and I realised that as soon as the fascination of your innocent blue eyes and hot little body had worn off. If you had showed any talent for entertaining a man I'd have put you to work.'

She turned crimson, then white. 'You make me sick!'

'Yes, I soon realised that I'd never get you to be sensible, and I don't like trouble or crying women. I didn't want you screaming for a policeman, either, or I'd have tried a little gentle persuasion.'

Ashen, she almost retched, her head bent, swallowing fiercely. She had half suspected what was in his mind, at the time, but she had told herself he wouldn't do that to her, that the rather unpleasant men he kept introducing her to were just people he worked with, and that the hints and jokes they made to and about her were just in bad taste. She had been too young to realise just what sort of world Roddy moved in!

'So when the chance came to vanish, without anyone looking for me, I took it. I'd left the bar, you see, around ten minutes before the earth-quake hit. I met a girl.' He grinned reminis-cently. 'She invited me to her place, around the corner. We had just got into bed when the place shook and she started screaming. When things settled down, we threw on our clothes and went out into the street. She had a brother who was a taxi-driver, who lived in the same flat. He drove us out of the city to some cousin of theirs who lived in the country in a shack. They said it would be safer where there were no tall buildings to fall on us. So we stayed there and got drunk on cheap local wine. I meant to come back to find out what had happened to you, but then I read about you in the papers, and discovered that I was supposed to be dead, so I thought . . . what the hell? Why go back and spoil a good ending? I settled down with my Mexican girl and started a new career making a sort of moonshine whisky, then I got bored with her, and I moved on to work with a Mexican firm as a surveyor.'

'You've been in Mexico all these years?' she asked incredulously, and he shook his head.

'I stayed there three or four years. That must be how come I missed your modelling career. I had no idea you'd been modelling. I had no idea you were rich or famous. And I certainly had no idea you had married again, and struck oil the second time around.'

Bitterly, Caitlin said, 'Or you would have been to see me before?'

'Not very nice!' he said, wagging a finger at her.

'But true!' she spat at him, her temper right out of control, and her blue eyes flashing.

He seemed amused, but put on a solemn air. 'If I had known where to find you, it's true that I would have made it my business to let you know that you'd committed bigamy and were facing a possible couple of years in prison. Not to mention the scandal.' He pretended to sigh, his face sober, except for his mocking eyes. 'I'm afraid it would whip up a lot of wicked gossip when it got out. I'm afraid Mr Ritchie is in for a very rough ride when the newspapers get hold of the story.' He eyed her with a pretence of concern. 'I suppose he will marry you again once we've been divorced?'

Her eyes flickered and she saw the satisfaction in his face, even as she was angrily saying, 'I'm not discussing him with you!'

'You're afraid he won't want you back once he knows, aren't you?' he jibed. 'Then we'd better make sure he doesn't know. I'll give you until Friday to come up with the twenty thousand.'

'I told you, I can't get hold of that sort of sum without arousing curiosity. I have a monthly allowance, but if I want anything expensive—jewellery or clothes—I charge it and the accountants pay the bills. Everything I buy goes into his damned computer. You don't understand; the money is all on paper, it isn't in my bank account.' She was feverish to make him understand and Roddy listened, scratching that blond stubbled chin with one brown finger.

She watched him and hated him, yet could understand why women looked at him with fascinated, excited eyes. He had a compulsive sexual attraction and his swagger, his selfish insolence and that deep inner coldness only made some women more infatuated. Caitlin was not one of them. She had been, once, but when that infatuation had died she'd learnt to hate him.

She had come to see what sort of man she had married long before the earthquake. For a short time Roddy had been charm itself to her; she had been wildly in love with him and they had had a long, sensual honeymoon on their trip by freightship to Mexico. She refused to remember their nights together during those first weeks. It hurt her to remember her utter abandonment to this man she now hated.

Once they'd reached Mexico, he had grown bored with her. The admission hadn't surprised her; she had known all about it at the time. He had slowly let his real self show. There had been moments of spite, even cruelty, times when he'd got drunk and hit her, times when he'd gone off with other women without bothering to conceal it. They'd had little money. Although his job had been well paid. Roddy had gambled, drunk, womanised the money away. They had soon owed the hotel a large sum and Caitlin had been forced to slink past the manager whenever she'd seen him coming. She had often had no money for food and had to go hungry to bed. She had been lonely, frightened and unhappy before the earthquake.

The real trauma, the scars she was left with afterwards, had come from her life with Roddy, not from the shock of being buried alive for days.

She had never talked about it, never dared. Talking about Roddy would have been to resurrect him, and she preferred him dead.

'You must sell some of your jewellery, then,' he said coolly. 'I know you've got plenty because I spent an hour this morning at a clippings agency, checking you and Mr Ritchie out. That's how I found out all about the modelling career.

Luckily, I happened to know a girl who works
in this clippings agency and she didn't charge me.
I read all about the diamonds and sapphires Mr
Richie loves to buy you. Sell a necklace or two.'

'I can't, without it being noticed! How could
I explain it?'

'You'll have to find a way,' he smirked.
'There's always a way, darling!'

Tears came into Caitlin's eyes. She looked at
him with incredulity. 'How can you do this to
me? Didn't you do enough in Mexico? I wish to
God I'd never met you. I hate you, you're the
most loathsome, disgusting——'

He caught hold of her arms, pinning her
against the park bench, and leant over her to
force his mouth down on to hers while she fought
and wept, sickened and in despair. He was mer-
ciless, ruthless, amoral; she had no chance of ap-
pealing to anything decent in him. If she paid
him this money, he would be back for more. If
she didn't, he would coolly destroy her life with
Monro and Gill. She would have to go away, and
the thought of that was what she cried for helplessly as she struggled.

He let go of her, grinning with self-satisfaction,
and Caitlin pulled a clean handkerchief out of
her jacket pocket and shakily wiped it backwards
and forwards over her mouth to rid herself of the
taint of his invasive mouth. Roddy watched her,
his grin hardening.

'Puritanical little bitch, aren't you? You
wanted it once, used to beg me to come to bed.
"Make love to me, Roddy," you used to

whimper, clinging all over me. I hate clinging women more than anything in the world. That was what really turned me off you; your reproachful, pallid little face, and the way you clung and cried.'

She ignored him, got up and threw the handkerchief into a litter bin nearby.

'I have to get back,' she said flatly, staring along the avenue of trees. An old lady with a spaniel on a lead was coming towards them. Caitlin watched the two approach without really noticing anything about them.

'I want the money by Friday,' Roddy said, getting up too. 'Friday, eleven o'clock, same place—the Food Hall at Harrods.'

She frowned. 'Why there again?'

'I want to be certain you aren't being followed,' he drawled.

The old lady passed them, giving Caitlin a shy smile which she somehow managed to return, although she had never felt less like smiling in her life.

'See you!' Roddy said abruptly, and Caitlin started, turning to look at him just in time to see him lope away through the trees, across the smooth lawn to vanish completely into another part of the gardens.

She sat down again and lapsed into melancholy, staring at the leaves on the nearest tree, watching the gentle fluttering as the wind moved through them, watching the changing reflection of sunlight from their veined surfaces. They were never still, never quiet; a soft murmur came from the tree all the time as if they were permanently commenting on everything they saw below them in the gardens.

She could not sell any of the jewellery Monro had given her. That would be theft. Monro had given them to her, that was true, and you could say they were hers, but she didn't feel that they were. They were family jewels. Monro had not given them to her to sell. He meant her to keep them, wear them when she performed her function as his wife. She was expected to look the part, always beautifully dressed, perfectly groomed, glittering like an icon with Monro's diamonds and sapphires around her throat, at her wrist, in her ears. That was part of the cool-headed bargain they had made.

Cool-headed—or cold-hearted? she thought bitterly, then sighed. Well, what difference did it make now?

How she felt about Monro had become irrelevant since Roddy had reappeared in her life. He was a human earthquake, erupting into her luxurious, settled world, blowing it to the four winds, altering the landscape forever.

She got up reluctantly and began to walk to the gates. She had to go back. She didn't want to because she knew that once she was home her troubles would begin. She would have to explain where she had been; she could be sure Austell would have told Monro that she had vanished without seeing the doctor. What was she going to tell him?

She stood outside the gates watching the traffic speeding past, waiting for a taxi. Her head ached; she couldn't think straight. She put a hand to her head, brows furrowed. She didn't know what she was going to say to Monro. That she had simply felt she must get out of the house? She had had a headache and needed some fresh air?

A taxi appeared with its sign illuminated to show it was free. She stepped off the kerb slightly, waving an arm to catch the driver's attention, and he pulled over to stop for her.

She gave him the address and climbed into the back of the cab. Leaning back in the corner, she closed her eyes, but that didn't help because she kept getting flashing images of things she did not want to dwell on...the earthquake, last night when she'd first seen Roddy again and incredulously recognised him, Gill hugging her tightly and saying, 'You'll never go away, will you, Caitlin?' Monro's face came and went, too, his eyes remote, his features forbidding. He would never forgive her for involving him in a huge public scandal. He hated seeing his name in print and went to great lengths to avoid journalists. He would be devastated to find himself in the most spiteful of the gossip columns.

Bigamy. An ugly word. Of course, she could plead total innocence, point to the legal declaration that Roddy was dead, protest that she had not known that he was alive...but who would believe her if Roddy put up his spicier story?

Would he, though? she frowned, staring at the shops they were driving past. His story accused her of complicity in fraud and bigamy, but only by implicating himself as well. If she was guilty, he was guiltier, and for attempting to cheat the insurance company he could be sent to prison. They could both be sent to prison! Roddy had to be bluffing. Why should he risk going to prison merely to get back at her for not paying his blackmail demands?

She let herself into the house with her key, without anyone hearing her, and slipped straight up to her bedroom. There was no sign of any of the servants, or of Monro. Perhaps he had not yet rung up? Or perhaps Austell had exercised his discretion, and not informed her husband of her absence? But the doctor must have been and gone—well, she could always ring him to apologise.

With a sigh of relief she went into her bathroom to take a shower. She had felt unclean ever since Roddy had touched her. She turned on the shower jet, shuddering at the memory of his mouth, and stripped off to step under the water. She would not feel clean again until she had scrubbed herself from head to foot.

She lathered herself copiously, rubbed shampoo into her hair, then stood under the shower with closed eyes, and let cool, cleansing water stream over her.

At last, she wrung her long blonde hair out, twisted it into a coil in the nape of her head, and put out a hand to grope for the towel she had hung just outside the shower cubicle.

The towel was put into her hand. She gave a gasp of shock; her eyes flew open, her damp lashes blinking as she looked into Monro's harsh face.

'Where have you been?' he bit out, and Caitlin pulled herself together, bent her head and wound herself hurriedly into the towel, her hands shaking as she wrapped it sari-like around her wet, nude body while Monro watched.

'I had to dash out, I'd forgotten something I had to do, something urgent ... a ... a committee meeting for the charity group Megan is organising ...' She was improvising stupidly; he could so easily ring Megan and ask her about this meeting. I can always ring Megan before he gets round to it, she thought. But what on earth will Megan think? Well, I know what she'll think. She'll laugh and welcome me to her little band of unfaithful wives, the adultery club who provide alibis for each other and swap anecdotes about their lovers while they have their hair done and their nails manicured. Caitlin had always rather despised them, and hadn't hidden it very well. Megan would be amused and rather triumphant.

She tried to edge past Monro, but he gripped her bare, wet arm, his fingers biting so deep that she knew she would have bruises there tomorrow.

'Who was the man who rang you just after I left?' he snarled, and taken aback she stammered again, knowing she sounded guilty but unable to stop herself.

'M...man...? Oh, Jeffrey, you mean? He just rang to ask how I was——'

'I spoke to Jeffrey,' Monro curtly told her. 'He didn't ring you at all this morning.'

She swallowed, very pale, a pulse beating visibly in her long neck. Monro watched it as if it was a witness against her.

'Now tell me the truth,' he said. 'Who was the man who rang you and gave Jeffrey's name? And why did you immediately get dressed and creep out without the servants having any idea you had gone?'

She took refuge in anger, pulling away from him, her head lifted and her blue eyes over-bright. 'Stop cross-examining me! I'm not one of your servants! I don't have to have permission to leave the house, surely? I had an important appointment, and I didn't want to spend the whole day in bed, pretending to be ill. I wasn't ill. There was no reason why I shouldn't go out if I wanted to.'

'Is there some reason why I can't be told where you went?' His voice was icy and she shivered.

'No, of course not.'

'Well?' he grated, glaring, and she glared back at him.

'I'd have told you if you'd asked some other way, but I won't be bullied as if I'm on trial for something.' She looked down at the hand still clamped on her arm, a livid whiteness around the pads of his fingers where they pressed down into her flesh. 'You're hurting. Let go!'

He shook her instead, and took hold of her other arm with as much violence. 'Who is he?' he asked thickly, leaning towards her. 'How long has it been going on? I'm going to find out sooner or later, so you might as well save yourself a lot of trouble by telling me now, and I want to know everything! Are you sleeping with him? How long has he been your lover? Do I know him?' At each harsh question he shook her mercilessly.

She was helpless in his grip, her head going backwards and forwards as he shook her, her long, wet hair slapping her bare shoulders. 'I don't have a lover! Please, Monro, stop...you're making me dizzy!'

He froze, but still held on to her and stared down into her agitated face, his cold grey eyes probing hers, his jawline taut. 'I've guessed for a long time that there was someone,' he said, and she was so startled that she could only gasp, staring back at him.

'Do you think I didn't realise you hated me to touch you?' he bit out. 'Or that I couldn't guess why? I knew there had to be someone else. I thought for a long time that you were still in love with that dead husband, but that was so long ago. I can't believe he's still haunting you. It has to be a living man who makes you so cold whenever I try to make love to you.'

Stung, she said, 'I've never refused to sleep with you!'

He laughed bitterly, his mouth twisting. 'Oh, no, you lay back and allowed me to do whatever I chose, but even when you seemed to be enjoying it I knew you were pretending, just to be polite. You kept your side of our bargain, I admit that. I have no right to complain. I didn't ask you to fall in love with me, or even to enjoy having sex—I just asked you to be my wife, look after Gill, run my home, and you did all three, perfectly. You're the perfect hostess, the perfect companion when we go out. All my friends envy me, and fancy you themselves like mad. Gill adores you and you've been wonderful to her. I'm very grateful to you for the way you've changed her life. I know you love her.'

'I do!' That, at least, she could answer with total honesty, and her voice was eager. Monro heard the eagerness and his eyes were grimly sardonic.

'But you can't stand the sight of me!'

Caitlin was too stunned to answer that for a moment. Did he really think she hated him? She began to stammer, 'I n-never said——'

'You don't have to say anything!' Monro ground out, brows drawn together. 'You made it pretty obvious. Why do you think I haven't been sleeping with you lately? My ego couldn't take any more of the sort of battering you've given it over the last year. No man likes to make love to a reluctant woman.'

Her nervous eyes flickered and lowered. She felt him watching her, then he said sharply, 'What happened to your ear?' He lifted a hand to the earlobe which had bled when Roddy had pulled the earring out of it, and she flinched, wondering how soon he would find out that her sapphire

and diamond earrings were missing. Monro
gently touched her earlobe with one finger,
frowning. 'The skin is torn. How did you do
that? You usually wear earrings—why aren't you
wearing any today?'

'I was,' she said huskily. 'I was wearing my
sapphire and diamond earrings when I went out.'
She hesitated, torn between lying and telling him
the truth, but she couldn't do that. She dared not
tell the truth, because the truth would be disastrous. 'I was mugged,' she said, feverishly in-
venting yet another lie. Did one more matter?
She had told him so many, some without even
knowing she was lying. She had told him her first
husband was dead—and Roddy was alive, and
that lie, innocently told in the beginning, was an
abyss between herself and Monro now. 'In the
street, outside Harrods,' she said. 'I was going
in to look for a present for Angela's birthday,
and someone just grabbed the earrings...he
wrenched them out of my ears, it hurt badly. It
bled, too. He was gone before I could even
scream. Nobody saw anything, and I was so
shocked I got a taxi back here without even going
into Harrods.'

Monro was frowning blackly. 'Didn't you tell
the police? You must report it, give them a des-
cripton of this mugger... What the hell is happening in this city? Right outside Harrods? You
were attacked right outside Harrods and nobody
tried to help you, or called the police? My God!
I'll call the police now.' He walked into her

bedroom and made for the phone beside her bed, and she ran after him in agitation, her face pale.

'No!'

Monro stopped still, eyes fixed on her face. 'Why not?' he asked in clipped tones.

'I...I didn't see him,' she stammered. 'One second he was there, grabbing my earrings, the next he was gone, and I have no more idea what he looked like than you do.'

Monro caught hold of her chin and tilted her face so that he could stare into her frightened, worried eyes.

His face was hostile, dangerous. He talked to her like an enemy, his voice savage. 'You were lying, weren't you? You weren't mugged. Who has your earrings? The lover you say you don't have?'

She put her hands up to push him away, and that was when he whipped her towel away. Caitlin gave a little groan and reached for it desperately; Monro held her wrists in an unbreakable lock.

Caitlin shut her eyes in dismay, as though the fact that she could not see him meant that he could not see her. It didn't help, of course. She might not be able to see Monro's face, but she could hear him breathing; she picked up the vibrations of his reaction to what he was staring at.

'Please...don't...' she whispered, tears burning behind her lids.

'Don't what?' Monro muttered thickly. 'Don't look at you? Don't touch you? Why shouldn't I do either? You're my wife and I have every right to look at you naked and touch you, and make love to you if I want to.' He took a long, harsh breath, 'And I do want to, damn you! You might have been doing it with your lover all morning, but now it's my turn.'

She went into panic, then, and found the strength to drag herself away and bolt for her bathroom, meaning to lock herself in there until he went away, but he caught her before she reached the door. His hands fastened on to her waist, slid round her and closed on her breasts, pulling her back against his body. She began to tremble violently. Monro held her like that for an instant, his mouth on the nape of her neck, his hands caressing her breasts, then without another word he picked her up and carried her over to the bed.

'Monro, for God's sake!' she pleaded, hardly daring to look at that set, forbidding face. He looked as if he was possessed by hatred. 'I couldn't bear it!' she burst out, meaning that she could not bear to have him make love to her in that angry mood, but he misunderstood, and snarled back at her.

'Well, that's too bad! You're going to have to bear it!' He dropped her on to the bed and began to take off his clothes with rough, fierce movements.

'No, I won't let you!' she almost sobbed, scrambling away from him to the other side of the bed. 'I don't want you to——'

'I don't give a damn what you want!'

He had shed his jacket, his tie, his shirt. He lunged over the bed to catch her by the ankles and drag her back towards him, anchoring her on the bed by climbing on top of her, his knees trapping her legs between them.

She lay still, like a mute, trapped little animal, staring up at him miserably as he knelt above her. He began to unzip his trousers and she made frantic, muffled little noises of protest, wordless protest, the whimpering of a snared rabbit which was hypnotised, intent on the approaching hunter, watching with enormous, dazed eyes as its fate came closer.

'We had a bargain,' Monro said thickly. 'I gave you my name, my money, my status, and my child to love—and you gave me your body. You've had what I promised you. Now give me what I want, and this time I don't expect a lifeless sacrifice. This time you aren't just lying there, pretending it isn't happening, politely opening your legs for me but giving nothing but submission. I'm going to have a flesh-and-blood woman in my bed for once. I want to hear you moaning when I'm inside you. I want you riding underneath me. I want passion from you this time, Caitlin.'

He was naked when he stopped muttering, and Caitlin was stricken into frozen silence now, staring at him, at the powerful chest, the black hair running downwards almost to his navel, at the lean hips and strong thighs. She was trembling violently. She felt as if she were a virgin, as if this were the first time a man had ever touched her. She wanted to hide from his eyes; they burnt her and they set her alight.

Monro didn't move for an instant. He knelt above her, watching her with glittering, narrowed eyes, his knees clasping her waist, his tanned body erect, aroused, hard with hot blood. She couldn't meet his eyes, but she felt them roving over her where she was sprawled on the bed, as he had flung her down. At last he did move, lazily stretched out a long index finger and flicked it across one of her breasts, watching the pink nipple harden and rise.

'You're beautiful,' he whispered. 'And you're my wife! It's time you learnt that.' Then his hands were touching her with tormenting sensuality, making her weak with yearning, making her afraid, because she had not wanted him like this before; she had not wanted any man like this since Roddy had died.

Her eyes clouded. Only Roddy was not dead. She had forgotten that. Monro's anger and passion had driven all thought of Roddy from her head.

'And you're my wife!' Monro said, but he was wrong. She was not his wife. She was another man's wife, and if she let him make love to her it would be adultery, but as Monro bent without haste to take her mouth she knew that she did not care whether or not they were legally married. That all seemed irrelevant now. His mouth was inches away and she watched it with a hunger that astonished her. She wanted him to kiss her. For years she had thought that all emotion had been burnt out of her by what she had suffered at Roddy's hands, yet she was feeling something now: a piercing need that made her stomach plunge.

She ran her hands up his chest slowly, sighing, her lips parting to meet the bruising demand of his mouth.

He had taught her to enjoy his lovemaking during the first months of their marriage. She had held aloof in his bed, it was true; but she knew that she had increasingly enjoyed the physical pleasure of his body, although she had never admitted it even to herself before now. He had taught her to want the pleasure he could give her, and she had missed it during the last few months when he had rarely come to her bed.

His rage seemed to have ebbed away. He was using another strategy against her now. He was teasing her, seducing her, his mouth exploring her eyes, her ears, kissing her neck, while his hands explored territory further down, tracing the delicate hollows of her throat and shoulders, cupping her breasts, softly wandering over her smooth, silky flesh, from breast to waist, over her rounded belly, her hips, down and down until his fingertips were stroking her inner thighs.

She gasped, arching, and his mouth came back to hers, a deep, possessive kiss which forced back her head and made her dizzy. She had her arms around him; she stroked his back and shoulders, feeling the muscles in them bunch as she touched him.

His mouth moved down from her lips to her throat, pressing kisses into the soft hollow at the base of it. He moved the kiss lower, lower, until he was kissing her breasts. His mouth parted a little, his tongue flicked out, like a snake, darted at her nipple, lazily licked round and round, until his open mouth closed on her breast and began to suck at it.

He had never done that before; she was startled, almost shocked, but at the same time piercing needles of excitement went through her. His head moved like a baby's in a rhythmic sucking first at one breast, and then at another, while she groaned weakly, driven almost mad with passion, raked her hands down his back, clenched her fingers in his hair, her thighs gripping him, her body writhing underneath his, deeply conscious of the hot pressure of his flesh close against her own.

Monro suddenly raised himself to stare down at her, his face hotly flushed and his eyes feverish.

Dazedly, Caitlin looked back at him, conscious that her long hair was tumbled all across the pillow, her skin as flushed as his, her breathing as rapid and uneven, her chest heaving, her body shaking.

'That's better,' he muttered in hoarse triumph. 'Now you look as if you've been making love! But we haven't even started yet, Caitlin . . . I want a lot more from you before I'm finished. First, you're going to tell me you want me. This time you are going to beg me to make love to you, not the other way around.'

Caitlin didn't understand at first; she lay under
him, her arms and legs wound round him,
staring, bewildered.

'Say it,' Monro grated. 'Tell me, beg.' He ran
his hand down her body and slid it between her
thighs; she felt a burning heat where it brushed
and tormented, and her eyes shut instinctively.
She gave a wild groan of pleasure and her body
arched up towards him.

'Say it,' Monro whispered huskily. 'I've got to
hear you admit you want me. You do, don't you?
This time you do.'

His heart was beating so fast that it made her
dizzy to feel it right above her, beating so hard
that it almost beat through her body too. She felt
the vibrations in her own chest.

'Yes, yes,' she muttered, pulling his mouth
down to her. 'I want you; make love to me...'

He was entering her while she was whispering
it; his body so urgent now that the thrust of his
entry made her cry out, jerking violently under
him. She looked up and saw his face set in a blind
mask of desire: his flesh drawn tightly over his
bones, his eyes closed, his mouth slightly open,
his breath coming sobbingly as he rose and fell
on top of her.

She didn't recognise him, he was a stranger.
He had never made love to her like this before;
his passion was so charged with anger that all her
own excitement drained away.

'Not like this!' she cried out in distress, but he
didn't even hear her. He was fast approaching a
climax, his breathing agonising, his body shud-

dering, his deep groans of pleasure and satisfaction making her almost hate him.

He collapsed on to her, and lay there, gasping, shuddering, breathing like a man rescued from drowning, then he rolled away and lay on his back, staring at the ceiling.

Caitlin scrambled off the bed and grabbed up a dressing-gown, pulled it round her and ran into the bathroom and locked herself in there. Crying silently, she turned on the shower and stepped under it again.

For the second time that day, she needed to scrub her body clean. For the second time that day a man had hurt her badly and left her hating him, and herself.

It was far worse this time, though, because Monro had hit her where she was most vulnerable—for a little while just now, in his arms, she had begun to feel, tentatively, that she might actually be falling in love with him. She had been so sure she would never love again, yet she had glimpsed the possibility of love on the horizon, almost within her reach, and she had felt a nervous little blaze of hope. She wanted to love. She needed to—she was no different from the rest of her sex; she needed human warmth, human contact, human emotions.

Monro had just killed that hope, though. He hadn't been making love to her; he hadn't been showing her a passionate emotion. She had wanted to believe he really loved her, that his anger was the rage of a man who was jealous because he was in love. Instead, it had been the fury of a man who thought someone else might be trying to steal one of his possessions, and who had decided to repossess it ruthlessly, stamp his brand on it. She was just a thing to him; she wasn't a woman, and he did not love her.

She wished she were dead.

CHAPTER FOUR

CAITLIN towelled herself roughly afterwards, as if scrubbing the taint of Monro's lovemaking off her body, then listened, ears pricked. She couldn't hear a sound. After hesitating briefly, she opened the door. The room was empty. He had gone, taking his clothes with him. The only sign that he had ever been there was the rumpled bed, and she averted her eyes from that, swallowing.

She ran to her bedroom door and locked it, then dressed with great haste in a plain white shirt and a straight black skirt. She swept her hair up on top of her head and put on make-up, surveying herself in the mirror with bitter distaste.

She wished she had been born plain. It was her looks that had ruined her life. If she did not have blonde hair, blue eyes and a good figure, Roddy wouldn't have chased her, she would not have been in Mexico with him, she wouldn't have become a model and later famous enough to catch Monro Ritchie's eye.

She should have been warned by the way he had behaved right at the beginning. He had sent George Abbot to get her with the cool arrogance of a man who believed he had the right to pick out a woman without even meeting her, and order her to be delivered to him. Gift-wrapped, no doubt!

He hadn't had marriage in mind in the beginning. She had known that; so had George Abbot. Monro had seen her and desired her, but if she had given in at the start he would never have married her. How many other women had he sent George to get for him, like a man pointing to a spaniel and ordering, 'Fetch!'?

By turning him down, holding out, she had forced him to marry her, although that had not been her intention. She hadn't wanted to know him, that was why she'd rejected all his approaches. Monro's ego hadn't been able to accept her indifference. She had been a challenge. He'd determined to get her, and eventually she had capitulated, but only because she had grown so fond of his little girl.

It hadn't occurred to her that her continuing indifference to him might have made Monro violently angry; she had been stupid.

His ruthless use of her had left her hating him, and facing the fact that she had to get away at once. Monro had not finished questioning her; he might have left, but he would be back and the cross-examination would start again. He believed she had a lover, and he would not give up until she gave him a name.

She couldn't tell him the truth. The truth would be even worse than the lie he had imagined.

She found a travelling case stowed on a shelf in her dressing-room and packed it with a few simple clothes. She would have no need of evening gowns or furs after this; she chose jeans and shirts, a couple of plain skirts, some underwear and nightdresses. All her jewellery was locked in a safe in Monro's study, but she would not have taken any of that anyway.

Life was going to be very different for her from now on; she would not be wearing jewels. She only took enough clothes to provide a basic wardrobe until she could get a job and earn enough to buy herself new things.

When she had closed the case she stood looking around the elegant, luxurious room, her face melancholy and ironic, then she glanced down at her left hand, at the engraved gold wedding-ring which was Victorian and had once belonged to Monro's grandmother, who had died not long before Caitlin had come into his life.

His grandmother had taken the ring from her hand a few hours before she had died and given it to him. 'Marry again,' she had told him. 'Choose the sort of girl who would like this ring, and you'll get the right girl.'

Monro hadn't told Caitlin that until after she had seen the ring and been touched by the way the gold had worn down with the years, the fine engraving faded and only just decipherable.

'My grandmother wore that for fifty years,' he had said, and she had gently traced the engraving with a fingertip.

'It's beautiful,' she had said.

'I'll buy you a new ring, of course,' he had said, and Caitlin had shaken her head.

'I'd prefer this! It might bring us luck to be married with your grandmother's ring.'

She had said the right thing, although she hadn't known it. Monro had told her later, not long before their wedding-day.

'I didn't want you to know before in case it swayed you. I wanted to be sure you really liked it.'

Would he have married her if she hadn't liked it? she wondered, slowly sliding the ring off her finger now and looking at it with tears in her eyes.

Leaving it behind seemed irrevocable, but she couldn't take it because it didn't really belong to her at all. She was not Monro's wife, and if she kept the ring she would be cheating both Monro and his grandmother, yet it made her intensely sad to leave the ring behind.

She picked up her case and went to the bedroom door, listening for a moment before she unlocked and opened it. There was no sign of anyone around. Gill would be at school. The servants would be in their own part of the great house. Monro...where was he? In his own bedroom? She was afraid of being caught before she could get out of the house, so she waited a while before tiptoeing across the landing. There was no sound from his bedroom, and the door was shut. She had no idea whether he was in there, or downstairs.

She crept down the stairs and froze as she heard the telephone ring. Austell answered it from the hall, his voice formal.

'Yes, sir, Mr Ritchie is here. One moment, please, sir.' She heard him put the telephone down and then heard the soft tread of his feet as he walked along the hall to Monro's study. Austell opened the door and went into the room; she picked up his quiet tones telling Monro that he was wanted on the phone and decided to make a dash for the front door.

She had put on low heels in case she had to run. She took the stairs silently, on the carpet, and then ran on tiptoe across the hall.

She kept expecting to hear an exclamation from either Monro or Austell, but there was only a low murmur of voices from the study as she reached the front door. She fumbled as she opened it, almost dropping her case, then she was out of the house, and carefully closing the door behind her so as not to alert anyone to her departure.

Once outside, she ran without looking back, and caught a taxi at the corner of the street.

Since her marriage, she had lost touch with most of the friends she had had during her career. They had not been close friends, anyway; it had usually been a matter of proximity in working together and once they no longer met at work they had ceased to have anything to say to each other. Added to that, some girls had been envious, others spiteful—and they had resented her marriage to a wealthy man like Monro.

Of all the models she had known, she had only continued to see two girls. One of them, Jasmine, an incredibly lovely Chinese girl, was in Hong Kong now. She was married, too, to a very rich Chinese importer. Jasmine wrote to Caitlin from time to time, but as she lived so far away they could only meet rarely.

The other girl still modelled, was still un-
married, and she lived in London. Natasha was
the only person Caitlin felt able to ask for help,
so she gave the taxi-driver the address of Joe
Fanucci's fashion house in Mayfair. She knew
that Natasha was working for Joe at present.

He was making his newest designs on her. Joe
liked to work with a live girl, often cutting the
material on her body just to see how the cloth
would fall when it was being worn. Joe liked
working with Natasha because she was an incredibly patient, sleepy girl, who could stand still
for hours without seeming to tire. She had olive
skin with a tan that looked like burnished gold,
hair of a coppery colour, lazy brown eyes, and
a body so lithe and plastic that he could almost
twist it into any shape he chose.

Somehow, she had never become a famous
model. Her face didn't fit on magazine covers,
nor did photographers queue up to use her, as
they had with Caitlin. But Natasha in her way
was a big success, in a very different field.

When Caitlin found her in the cutting-room
that afternoon, she was standing like a rock in
the middle of a maelstrom. Joe was there, flinging
a bolt of tawny-orange silk about with angry ges-
tures. His head cutter, Jason, was there, spitting
like a cat over something. His head *vendeuse* was
there, too, reading a list of customers to him in
a piercing, insistent voice. Madame Lestrade was
as French as Soho, where she had been born. She
had trained in Paris with Dior and she treated
Joe with contempt, which he enjoyed. She also

treated his customers with arrogance, which he encouraged, since it overawed most of them.

'And none of these bills have been paid!' Madame Lestrade icily informed Joe. 'You cannot run a house like this! If they don't pay us, how are we to pay our creditors? You must deal with it at once.'

'Yeah, yeah. Tomorrow, OK?' Joe said, waving her away. 'Jason, what is it with you? This silk is going to cut like butter.'

'It will disintegrate,' Jason spat. 'Look at the stuff! Where did you get it? It will take twice as much material for each unit—how often have I told you? Buying cheap never pays.'

'Cheap? You call this cheap? This is Chinese silk!'

'Cheap Chinese silk, from Hong Kong,' Jason said scornfully.

Natasha suddenly spotted Caitlin and broke into a smile, wiggling her fingers in greeting.

'Keep still!' Joe roared, turning on her. 'You've broken the line! If I make a mistake and Jason cuts this badly, I'll kill you!'

'I have never cut badly!' Jason screamed, waving his scissors at Joe, who made matters worse by sneering,

'Never? Please!'

Jason began to have hysterics.

'It's my fault,' Caitlin said, and everyone looked round in surprise. Joe dropped the tawny silk and came over with outstretched arms.

'Caitlin, sweetie! How are you? Kiss kiss.' He touched his face to hers, first one cheek, then the other, French style, then held her away and gazed at her with narrowed eyes. 'Don't tell me...the Renoir dress was a failure? His Eminence, your legal lord, didn't like it? I heard you made a little scene at the exhibition. Fainting, forsooth!' He raised an eyebrow wickedly. 'Not anticipating a happy event, are we?'

Caitlin forced a smile, shaking her head. 'Nothing like that. And the dress was a big success, Joe. Everyone adored it and wanted to know who made it.'

'And you told them, I hope?'

'Of course,' she smiled. 'You should get lots of new customers from last night.'

He glowed. Of Italian stock, but American birth, Joe Fanucci was very dark, with olive skin, black eyes, and black hair, which he wore rather long in defiance of the current fashion for shorter hair.

He was slightly built, not very tall, and would no doubt one day put on weight if he went on eating pasta the way he did, but for the moment he was still slim and very attractive. He made his own clothes, although he preferred designing for women, and today he was looking particularly good in a cream linen suit, the jacket of which he had abandoned to work in shirtsleeves and a very tight, tailored waistcoat which made his waist look extremely small.

He was temperamental, but that he hid from his customers. Only his models knew how Joe could rage if things went wrong. He was an emotional man, and a nice one with a warm heart. Caitlin had always been fond of him.

Monro disliked him intensely, but that was probably only because he resented the fact that she had once worked for Joe and knew him well. Monro preferred her to distance herself from all her old friends, but as far as Joe and Natasha were concerned she had taken her own line, and she was glad of it now.

'Joe,' she said, 'can I have a word with Natasha alone? I won't keep her long.'

'OK,' he said amiably. 'But she can't move. I'm halfway through trying something out on her and I don't want to spoil the shape. Talk to her here; we'll all go and get a coffee and be back in five minutes. Want a coffee, Caitlin?'

'No thanks,' she said, then looked at Natasha. 'But Tasha might——'

Joe gave her an amazed look. 'Not while she's modelling! You've been away from it too long, Caitlin. You'll forget your own name next!'

'Sorry,' she said, grimacing, and he and the others left the long, stark room which was something like an artist's studio: bare floorboards, lots of windows and a skylight overhead, long, narrow tables laid down the centre of the room for cutters to work at. Bolts of material were piled up on shelves around the room; all the colours of the rainbow, but filtered through gauzy clouds of butter muslin which had been thrown over them to keep off the dust.

'What's wrong, Caitlin?' asked Natasha shrewdly, her very large brown eyes open to their extreme width.

'I can't tell you all of it now, but I need help, Tasha.' She gave the other girl a pleading look. 'Could I stay with you for a day or two until I sort myself out?'

Natasha pursed her lips, staring, then gave a low whistle. 'You've walked out on Monro?'

She nodded. 'I could go to a hotel if it isn't convenient, but——'

'Hotel? Nonsense. Of course you'll stay with me. My handbag's over there, on that chair. Hand it to me.'

Caitlin looked round, identified the small white handbag and brought it to her. Natasha hunted through it and found a key-ring. She detached a key from it.

'This is my spare, you can keep that for as long as you need to use the flat. Let yourself in, make yourself at home. I should be back at around seven tonight, if I'm lucky and Joe gets tired by six. He's been at it since eight this morning, and I happen to know he has a dinner party this evening, so I should get off work on time. If you want to go out, though, don't bother to wait in for me. Treat the place like a hotel. You're very welcome.'

'Thank you,' Caitlin said gratefully. 'I really appreciate this, Tasha. Do the same for you one day.'

'My pleasure,' Natasha said, with a friendly grin.

Caitlin hesitated. 'And . . .'

'Yes?' Natasha watched her curiously.

'I hate to ask this, but if Monro comes here, asking if you've seen me, could you——'

'Tell him we haven't?' guessed Natasha. 'Trust us.'

'Will you tell the others? I'd rather not get into a discussion about why——'

'Don't worry, they'll understand. Hey, look! Marriages run into these sticky patches. A few days, and you'll feel better about whatever's bugging you.'

Caitlin smiled wearily. 'Sure.'

Joe and the rest of the troupe came back noisily, squabbling, and Caitlin said goodbye and left. She got another taxi after waiting for a few minutes on New Bond Street, a stone's throw from Joe's place.

She had been to Natasha's flat many times before. She had even shared it with her briefly not long before she had married Monro. It gave her an odd sensation, though, letting herself in at the front door and looking around the tiny flat. It was only two years since she had moved from this world to Monro's very different life-style—yet she knew that she was a very different person now, and she wondered wryly how she was going to adapt back to living this way.

Natasha's flat was in Camden, on the north side of London, just below Hampstead Heath. It was on the very top floor of a four-storey Victorian house overlooking a narrow canal. The ceilings were sloping and rather low, the windows tiny. Natasha had furnished it with an eclectic clutter of things she had bought in junk shops and on market stalls.

The furniture was old and shabby, but had been polished until it shone. The curtains were gay poppy-red in the sitting-room, the walls painted gloss white. There were pictures everywhere, mostly by young people at art school in London, whose work Natasha had bought cheaply at Camden Market, or been given by the artist if it happened to be a friend of hers. A lot of art students lived in lodging houses around Camden and frequented local coffee houses and cafés in the evenings and at weekends.

At one end of the room was a minute kitchen/dining-room. Along a wall ran a pine-wood worktop with a sink and ceramic hobs set in it. There were cupboards above and below it, and it also served as a breakfast bar with two chrome stools neatly positioned next to it.

Caitlin made herself a cup of tea and sat down with it to review her situation. What was she going to do?

She couldn't stay in London for more than a day or two because, even if Joe and the others lied to Monro when he came looking for her, as he was certain to do sooner or later, it wouldn't take him long to track her down to this flat. He knew Natasha was one of the few friends she had kept from her old life. He would be bound to work out that she would have gone to Natasha for help.

After all, she could hardly go to one of his friends, could she? And all the friends she had made since their marriage had been made through Monro, were mutual friends of them both. They were the last people she would ask for help now, and Monro knew it.

Joe could help her to get some sort of work—not as a model, now. She was too old for that and, anyway, she did not want a job which would bring her into the limelight. Monro must not find her.

She sat there, sipping her tea, and puzzling over her problem for some time, then unpacked and put her things away in Natasha's boxlike spare bedroom. It was just big enough to hold a narrow bed and a thin, high chest of drawers. Caitlin had to hang her skirts and jeans up from a brass rail Natasha had installed along the wall as a substitute wardrobe.

Natasha arrived a little while later, flushed from her nightly tussle on the Northern Line of London's underground railway. It was a busy line, and often quite dangerous—muggers and drug addicts frequented it late at night—but at this time of day it was merely crowded with the travellers packed into each compartment like sardines in a can. You had to fight your way on and fight your way off.

Natasha flopped down in an old rocking-chair she had re-covered herself with poppy-red cotton left over from the curtains. She kept the chair piled with fat cushions in basic colours: vivid green and blue and yellow.

'Give me five mintues to get my breath!' she gasped, rocking. 'Then I'll get us some supper.'

'I thought we might eat out,' Caitlin suggested. 'The new Italian place on the corner looks good.'

'Expensive,' said Natasha warningly.

'My treat!'

Natasha lifted her brows. 'You didn't run out on Monro without your cheque-book, then?'

'I'm not hard up,' agreed Caitlin drily. She had quite a large amount in her private account from her modelling days and she would not need to use any of Monro's money.

'Well, that would be great, then,' Natasha said with an expression between yearning and wistful regret. 'But I have to watch my diet, you know. Still, they probably do a grilled sole and salad.'

They did, and both girls ate that, after melon served with wafer-thin slices of Parma ham. Then they had fresh fruit salad, a delicious mixture of peaches, strawberries, raspberries and grapes.

Their talk was light and frothy, largely gossip about mutual friends and the fashion world. They laughed and chattered and kept away from anything serious. Natasha didn't ask any questions about the sudden rift between Caitlin and Monro, and Caitlin didn't volunteer any information. She couldn't face the idea of telling anyone that she had unwittingly committed bigamy. Natasha would be sympathetic, but even sympathy would be painful.

They were at the coffee stage when Monro walked into the restaurant. Caitlin was facing the door. Her cup halted halfway to her mouth and she went pale.

'So I said, "Go jump in a pond!" and I won't repeat what he said to that!' said Natasha blithely, unaware of Caitlin's rigidity.

Caitlin was so startled that she couldn't even look away from his frowning face. He was furious, and wasn't hiding it. A nervous pulse began beating in her neck. How on earth had he tracked her down?

The other customers were staring too. Not because they recognised Monro, but because he looked out of place in this casual little local restaurant. He was wearing an evening suit and a black evening cashmere coat; a white silk scarf hung round his neck, swinging slightly as he walked towards them. Caitlin vaguely remembered that he had mentioned a large dinner party for that evening. He must have gone alone.

How had he found her so quickly? Had Joe talked? She had been sure she could trust Joe, but who else could have told Monro where she was?

She was scared he would make a scene, and if he was going to be difficult it would be better to get out of the restaurant first, so she muttered, 'Can we go, Tasha?'

Natasha looked surprised. 'I haven't drunk my coffee yet. Are you tired? We'll go in a minute. Shall we get the bill? Where's that waitress? She was here a minute ago...' Her voice tailed off as Monro halted beside the table. 'Oh!' Her eyes flew to Caitlin's face, anxiety in her glance.

'Good evening,' Monro said in icy courtesy, bowing his head towards Natasha while his stare stayed fixed on Caitlin's stricken face.

'Oh, hello, Monro,' Natasha said uncertainly.

'I've come to collect my wife,' he said to her, still staring at Caitlin.

'Oh, I see,' Natasha said, at a loss to know what else to say. She looked questioningly at Caitlin, who avoided her glance.

'I am staying with Natasha,' Caitlin said.

'You're coming home!' There was a leashed impatience in his voice, in the glitter of his eyes.

'No. I'm not.' Her chin lifted, a stubborn determination in her face. She picked up her cup and sipped some more coffee. 'Go away, Monro, and leave me alone.'

The leash snapped. He lost control of his temper and grabbed her arm roughly. 'You are coming home with me!'

Caitlin was still holding her coffee-cup; she didn't stop to think. She just threw it at him. Monro ducked in an instinctive reflex action. The coffee didn't hit his face, which she had been aiming at, but it splashed his shirt and jacket, and all around them people stared and whispered, some of the younger ones starting to laugh.

Natasha's jaw dropped. She eyed Caitlin with astonished respect. 'I didn't think you had it in you! Go on, knock him out now!'

Caitlin gave a semi-hysterical giggle. She didn't quite believe herself that she had had the nerve to do that.

Monro's face was savage; he glared at her and at Natasha, then snatched up a napkin from the table and wiped his jacket, scowling.

The head waiter came bustling up, very agitated and lapsing into menacing Italian, waving his hands about.

Caitlin didn't speak Italian, yet she picked up the general drift of what he was saying. He wanted them to leave, but first he wanted to be paid. He had their bill in his hand and waved it at them.

Caitlin got up to go, reaching for the bill, but Monro got there first. He snatched it, looked at it, then pulled out his very fat wallet and the waiter's face changed. He stopped scowling. Monro dropped a pile of notes on to the table and the head waiter started beaming. Caitlin felt sick.

She walked to the door with Natasha hurrying after her. The head waiter scuttled round them and pulled the door open, bowing them all out.

'Creep!' Natasha told him as she walked out. Caitlin ignored the man, and so did Monro.

The Rolls-Royce stood at the kerb. It was empty, so Monro was for once driving himself. Perhaps he did not want their chauffeur to witness whatever happened tonight? There must be plenty of gossip going on among the servants already. No doubt he did not want to give them anything else to whisper about. What had he expected to see when he caught up with her? Or rather, who had he expected to see?

The head waiter stood at the door admiring the Rolls and watching his departing customers with curious eyes. Had he recognised Monro, whose face was often on the city pages and sometimes in the society gossip columns too? Caitlin hoped not. He might pass on the anecdote to the Press if he had recognised them.

She started off towards the flat with Natasha hurrying along beside her. 'I hope he isn't going to turn nasty,' Tasha whispered. 'I don't like scenes, especially in the street. I have a very low embarrassment threshold.'

'I'm sorry you got caught up in this!' Caitlin wished she had gone to a hotel after all. She had had no right to involve Natasha in her private problems.

'Hey, look! Forget it! What are friends for?' Natasha sounded jokey, but her eyes were serious and concerned.

Monro was at their heels. 'You are coming home, Caitlin!' he said fiercely, as they reached the house in which Natasha had her flat. He gripped her wrist in an unbreakable hold, his fingers cruel.

She didn't struggle this time. She ignored him, looking at Natasha as calmly as she could. 'You go up to the flat, Tasha. I'll see you later.'

'Look, Caitlin, I'll stay if you need me!' Natasha said.

'You heard what she said!' Monro bit out, glaring.

She glared back. 'Yes, and I've watched you bullying her, too. If you ask me——'

'I didn't!'

Natasha rode over his interruption. 'If you ask me, she needs a bodyguard!'

'You don't know anything about this, so mind your own business!' he grated.

'Please...Tasha...' Caitlin broke out miserably. 'Thanks for wanting to help, but I'll be OK. Go up to the flat, I won't be long.'

Natasha stared at her uncertainly. 'Sure you'll be OK?'

'Don't worry about me,' Caitlin said, and Natasha went at last, her face reluctant, leaving Caitlin confronting Monro at the door.

He let go of her wrist and stood there silently for a moment, as if suddenly finding it difficult to know what to say. She lowered her lashes and watched him through them, aching.

'I'm sorry I lost my temper and threw the coffee,' she said unsteadily.

'So I should damned well think. This shirt will never be the same again.'

'Well, I'm sorry about that, but you manhandled me once too often today!' she snapped back, and his brows drew together.

'Don't push me too far, Caitlin! My temper's on a hair-trigger tonight, I warn you.'

'When isn't it? Don't try to bully me, Monro! I'm in no mood to stand for it. Anyway, how did you find me? Who told you where I was? Not Joe?'

His face darkened with angry blood. 'No, Joe Fanucci didn't tell me anything, but I know you were with him this afternoon, so don't bother to lie about that. I had a private detective following you——'

'You what?' she gasped, too incredulous at first to be angry.

He shrugged, frowning. 'I arranged it this morning, when you first vanished from the house. I was worried about you, after that faint last night. They picked you up the second time you went out. You went from my bed straight to him, didn't you?' His voice was hoarse with rage. 'Couldn't you wait to tell him what had happened? My God, when I think of you pouring it all out to him...it makes my stomach turn over!'

'I haven't told Joe anything! Do you think I'd really talk about...about what you did to me this afternoon?'

'What I did? I made love to you, that's what I did! I made love to my own wife! Why the hell should I apologise for that?'

She stared into his grey eyes and they moved restlessly away, his face tightened, his mouth twisting.

'There wasn't much love involved, Monro,' she said flatly.

His eyes flashed back to her face; he was so tense that she could almost see the bones thrusting through the taut mask of his skin.

'So you admit it. It's him, isn't it? I guessed long ago. Fanucci has always been hanging around in the background, hasn't he? Was he your lover before we were married, or did it start afterwards?'

She was stunned into silence, staring back and meeting the icy, watchful hostility of his stare. Swallowing, at last she stammered, 'J...Joe isn't m...my lover! He's just an old friend!'

Monro laughed cynically. 'Oh, sure! Of course he is!'

'It's true!' she burst out, trembling. 'I might have known I couldn't expect someone like you to understand. Sex is all you expect from a woman, isn't it? You've never tried talking to a woman, making friends with one. Women aren't people to you! They're things, status symbols, like your Rolls or your personal jet. You send George Abbot out to get you one when you feel the urge for sex, that's all, like someone sending out for a pizza or a Chinese take-away. You sent him out for me because you noticed my face on a magazine cover. If I'd been willing, you would have slept with me—how often? How many times do you usually sleep with your pick-ups, Monro? Once? Twice? Three times? Well, they aren't long-term affairs, after all. Just junk sex. Use them and throw them away.'

He stood there, white-faced, his body rigid as he listened, and he made no attempt to interrupt now, or to silence her. Not that she would have let him stop her. She had had this boiling inside her ever since Geroge Abbot had come to see her and made it clear what his employer wanted of her. She had never been brutally frank with Monro before, but he had it coming, and he was going to hear it all.

'You think I don't know how you see me?' she asked bitterly. 'I'm just one of your possessions, aren't I? I wouldn't go to bed with you in the beginning, so you had to marry me, which was a higher price than you normally pay the women you use, but having paid so much for me you aren't ready to let me walk out just yet. Haven't you had your money's worth yet, Monro?'

'Stop talking like that!' he said harshly, staring down at her. 'I've never seen you as a possession——'

'No? Then why did you have me followed by a private detective?'

'I had to know who you were seeing! I couldn't sleep, wondering if you were having an affair with Fanucci. I told you . . . I know there's someone else.'

She drew a long, shaky breath. Sooner or later, he would have to know about Roddy, but she was too tired to tell him tonight. She had had enough for one day. She could not face telling Monro now.

'Please, Monro, leave me alone,' she said wearily. 'It's late and I'm tired; I just want to get some sleep.'

'Come home with me, then. We can talk in the morning,' he said, his voice gentler. 'Caitlin, we have to talk if we're going to save our marriage . . .'

Her eyes burned with unshed tears. She was too distraught to be wary of how she phrased it, she just threw it at him roughly. 'Our marriage is over.'

He stared down into her face, trying to read the bitter play of emotions raging over it. 'Over?' he repeated dully. 'Just like that? Suddenly, our marriage is over, without explanation, warning, anything?'

'Oh, please, just let me go,' she said, trying to dart past him into the house.

He caught her arm, his fingers violent, wrenching her round to face him again, and bent towards her, talking thickly.

'I'll never let you go, Caitlin! Not in a million years! You're mine, and I'm going to keep you, do you hear?'

She was trembling, her breathing fast and painful. 'You're hurting me!' she whispered through white lips, and Monro frowned, then abruptly released her.

'All right, spend tonight with Natasha, but I want you home again tomorrow morning, or I'll come to fetch you.'

He turned on his heel and strode away, the chilly night wind catching his white silk scarf and his black hair, blowing them both about. Caitlin watched him with tears welling up in her eyes.

Tomorrow she would have to move on before Monro came looking for her. She had hoped to spend a few days with Natasha while she looked around for a new home, a new job, but she had been over-optimistic. Monro had caught up with her faster than she had anticipated. She hadn't known about the detective he had trailing her.

She heard the slam of the car door, then the flare of the engine, and the Rolls-Royce moved off around the corner. The sound of the engine died away and Caitlin still stood there, thinking feverishly.

Was the detective still watching her? She looked around warily, eyes alert for any movement, any sign. He could be anywhere—in a parked car, hiding in a shop doorway, watching her from a garden.

She shuddered. It was a horrible sensation, knowing that you were being watched by a total stranger in hiding, that you could do nothing without it being recorded and reported to your husband.

Did the detective know about the back entrance to the house in which Natasha had a flat, though? There was a garden behind the house, and at the rear of the garden a fence with a gate in it which led out into an alley running parallel to this road.

She would get up at first light and pack, take a plane somewhere. She didn't care where she went, so long as she could get a long way away from Monro.

CHAPTER FIVE

CAITLIN found Natasha making hot chocolate. Looking over her shoulder anxiously, Tasha asked, 'Are you OK?'

Caitlin gave her a rather forced, wry smile. 'I'll survive.' She accepted the steaming mug Natasha held out. 'Thanks. Tasha, I'm moving on early tomorrow morning. I'll be gone before you're up, I expect. Thanks for putting up with me.'

Natasha watched her thoughtfully. 'Going back to him?'

Caitlin shook her head.

'Then what?'

'I think it would be best if you don't know my plans,' Caitlin said, and Natasha looked offended.

'I wouldn't give you away to your husband, you know!'

'I'm sure you wouldn't, but if he even suspects that you know something he won't leave you alone. If you really don't know anything, you'll be much more relaxed when you see him, and he'll soon realise that and give up on you.'

Natasha made a face. 'Shrewd. I suppose you're right.' She frowned. 'Is your marriage finished, Caitlin? Aren't you ever going back?'

'Never,' said Caitlin, hearing the melancholy echoes of the word inside her head. She looked at the clock. 'It's late, I must get to bed or I'll never get up early enough tomorrow morning. Goodnight, Tasha. Thanks for everything.'

'You're not going to vanish forever, are you?' Natasha said, frowning. 'We'll hear from you when you've settled somewhere? There aren't many girls I've kept in touch with over the years, just you and a couple of others. I'd hate to lose sight of you for good.'

'I'll be in touch,' promised Caitlin, at the door of the tiny bedroom. 'Goodnight, Tasha.'

She didn't think she would sleep, but she was so exhausted, both emotionally and physically, that she fell asleep almost at once, and when her alarm went off she jumped up in shock from a deep sleep, her nerves jangling.

It was six o'clock; the sky was a pale, livid grey. Somewhere on the edge of London the sun was rising, colouring the horizon with running streaks of flame. Caitlin didn't draw the curtains, but she carefully peered through the centre of them to check on the street outside. Now that it was daylight she could see inside most of the parked cars, and there was no sign of anyone in one. Of course, there might be someone lying down on the seat, but there was nobody in sight.

She had repacked her case and laid out her clothes. All she had to do was take a quick shower and dress. She drank a cup of instant coffee and ate a peach, then tiptoed out of the flat. Natasha would still be fast asleep and she didn't want to wake her.

She let herself out at the back, walked quietly to the gate in the fence, and slipped through into the alley. A quick glance and she still didn't see anyone watching her, but she started running.

Several streets away, she saw an early morning workmen's bus heading towards her, and sped across the road to catch it. It took her as far as King's Cross Station, and there she walked through the main-line station and picked up a taxi to Heathrow Airport.

She sat in the terminal studying the departure boards. There were flights going to most of the European capital cities, and she was tempted by the idea of Italy, largely because she had never been there with Monro. She did not want to go anywhere she had been before. Monro was going to be looking for her, she could be certain of that, and she wanted to throw him off the track as much as possible, so it had to be somewhere unlikely, somewhere he would not associate with her.

She went to the Air Italia desk and tried to book a seat on the Rome flight, but it was fully booked that morning. There was a flight to Venice later, but she was afraid of Monro dispatching someone to the airport to watch for her. She wanted to get away soon.

Her eye roamed helplessly over the names of cities and halted at Málaga in Spain. Spain! she thought. She had once told Monro she didn't like Spain—she was very disturbed by bullfighting, and the Spanish resorts were always full of

drunken English tourists causing havoc and of-
fending the Spaniards.

He would never think of looking for her there!
She walked over to that desk and, as if it had
been meant, there was a seat available on an early
flight. She booked on to it and an hour later was
in the departure lounge waiting for her flight to
be called.

A woman sitting opposite her was carrying
several plastic bags. Caitlin suddenly noticed that
one of them bore the name 'Harrods'. She bit
her lip, a thought striking her. Roddy had told
her to meet him on Friday morning with the
twenty thousand pounds in the Food Hall at
Harrods.

What would he do if she didn't turn up?

Her mind began working like crazy, coming
up with a terrible scenario. If she didn't show up
at Harrods, Roddy would ring her, and she
wouldn't be there. Monro would have been
hunting for her for days by then. Any phone-call
for her would be monitored and checked out.
Monro would find Roddy.

She winced. No, how could he? He couldn't
have a phone-call tapped and tracked back to a
place! Only the police could do that. But what
if Monro called in the police? After all, she was
the wife of an extremely wealthy and important
man. Her disappearance might be treated as
suspicious.

But what if Roddy, discovering that she had
run away, decided to blackmail Monro instead?

If he needed money that badly he wouldn't hesitate.

She should have warned Monro before she had left. She should have written to him to explain, as she found it so hard to tell him face to face that they were not really legally married. She looked at the clock. Another ten minutes before her flight was called. She should just have time to write him a brief note, explaining, warning him about Roddy and possible blackmail.

She had some writing paper in her travelling case. She got out a sheet and began to write. There was no time to wrap it up in careful words. She told him what had happened over the past couple of days and explained why she was going. She ended by telling him not to give Roddy money—it would just mean that he would never be rid of him.

Be careful, Monro, she wrote. Roddy is a parasite, but he is a vicious one. Take care when you're dealing with him.

Her flight was called as she signed her name. She slid the paper into an envelope, stuck a stamp on it and ran over to a post-box to send it before joining the end of the queue as passengers filed out of the lounge.

Sending that letter to Monro had cleared her mind to some extent. She had been so afraid he would find out, yet now that she had told him she felt much easier. There was nothing more to be afraid of now. She need not fear Roddy. Monro would deal with him, she could be sure of that. She didn't know how Monro would do it, but she was certain he would not let Roddy leech on to him.

Men like Monro knew how to protect themselves, and their money. That was why they were where they were. They were survivors, as tough as shoe leather. They had had to be, to claw and fight their way to the top, and stay there.

She wasn't tough, but she was a survivor, she thought drily. She had somehow lived through a humiliating and degrading life with Roddy, through that earthquake and being buried alive, through the strain and pressure of a job as a top model, and through marriage to one of the richest men in the world.

She might be very female and very vulnerable—but she had a vein of strength hidden somewhere to draw on when she needed it, and she meant somehow to live through this latest crisis in her life. Roddy's resurrection might have wrecked her life, but she would get over that one day. She didn't know how, but she had faith in herself as a survivor.

The only thing preying on her mind as she flew on her way to Spain was the possibility that Monro would find her before he had read that letter and realised that they had never legally been married anyway.

Monro wouldn't set the police on her trail because that would be embarrassing for him, and might alert the Press to her disappearance. No, he would use his own private resources. He would have private detective agencies all over the world looking for her, checking out hotels, railway stations, airports.

Airports. She had had to use her own name and address to book her flight this morning because she had had to produce her passport before boarding the plane. That would register on the airline's computer, and Monro would soon discover where she had gone, she thought grimly.

He would have his men combing the Spanish coast until they found her, and it wouldn't be hard because she would have to stay in a hotel, and hand in her passport. Once Monro's detectives had traced her to Málaga they would soon find her hotel.

'A drink, madam?' asked the air stewardess, and she blinked, turning dazed eyes on the woman.

'Sorry?'

'A drink from the bar, madam?' the stewardess repeated.

Caitlin shook her head, then changed her mind. 'Do you have any orange juice?'

'Certainly, madam.' She was served with chilled orange juice from a can and drank it thirstily. She hadn't eaten that morning, but she felt sick anyway. She refused the plastic meal she was offered, but did eat a bread roll which wasn't inedible. It settled her stomach to some extent, but dwelling on the chance of Monro turning up in Spain in search of her made her feel sick again a few minutes later.

With any luck he would get her letter before he decided whether or not to come to Spain in search of her. Once he knew they were not really married at all, he would no longer bother. He didn't love her. He merely saw her as his property because she bore his name. With her gone and the truth out in the open, he would simply marry someone else and forget her.

She closed her eyes. She wished she had had a chance to say goodbye to Gill. She was going to miss the girl badly, and she knew Gill would miss her. That was one good thing that had come out of her disastrous marriage—her relationship with Gill. The child was an important part of her life now, and she was miserable at leaving her.

'Feeling nervous?' asked the man in the next seat, and Caitlin opened her eyes reluctantly. He was short, middle-aged, balding, and he had been staring at her for some time.

'A little.' It wasn't true, of course, but she wasn't telling him the truth. The lie would serve. She didn't like the look of him.

He smiled patronisingly. 'Never flown before? Never mind, you'll be fine. It's safer than crossing the road, you know.' He patted her knee, sweat on his upper lip. 'I'll look after you. First time in Málaga? Where are you staying? Maybe we could meet up there.'

'My husband's meeting me,' Caitlin said coldly, and closed her eyes again. He didn't bother her for the rest of the journey.

When they landed at Málaga, she took a taxi to a good hotel and was lucky enough to get a room for the night. Málaga was a large town beside the sea and her hotel was on a busy main road near the harbour. Opening the window, she listened to the roar of traffic, and decided to close the window again. She hoped she was going to sleep that night.

After she had rested for an hour she went for a walk through some handsome shopping streets, looked at the ships in the harbour, admired a very beautiful public park nearby, but decided that she did not want to stay there for longer than a day or two. She took a taxi to the railway station and considered the various destinations before picking Marbella as the next stop on her flight.

Going by train would make it much harder for Monro's detectives to pick up her trail. You didn't have to show your passport when you bought a train ticket, or even use your name. You could be anonymous.

'Hello, again!'

The voice made her jump. She turned, going pale, and then relaxed when she saw that it was only the bald man from the plane.

She gave him a cold nod and walked away, but he wasn't to be shaken off that easily. He kept up with her.

'Didn't you find your husband? Going on from here by train, are you? I know Spain very well, lived here on and off for years. Maybe I could help if you have a problem?'

Caitlin stopped. 'No, thank you. I don't need your help. Excuse me, please.'

She walked on. He kept step beside her, talking coaxingly. 'How about a drink before dinner? I'm here on my own, so are you—it seems meant, doesn't it?'

Caitlin saw a Spanish policeman advancing towards them. She turned to confront her persecutor. 'Do I have to call that policeman before you'll leave me alone?'

The bald man grimaced. 'No need to turn nasty! I was only being friendly.'

'I don't need a friend. Please go away!' Caitlin hurried away and this time he didn't follow her. She went back to her hotel and had a shower because walking in the hot summer afternoon had left her flushed and sticky with perspiration. Half an hour later, cool and refreshed, she lay on her bed reading some brochures on local places of interest that she had picked up from the hotel desk, and was fascinated by one glossy folder on the city of Granada and the Moorish palace of the Alhambra.

She had often thought of visiting the Alhambra, and here she was, just a few hours' drive away. It seemed a pity to miss the opportunity. She picked up the phone and rang the hotel desk. They were only too happy to arrange for her to take a coach trip to the Alhambra, the next day.

The coach picked her up at her hotel quite early in the morning. She had had a good night's sleep followed by a light breakfast of rolls, jam and coffee, and was feeling rather better. The coach was half empty, so she managed to get a seat by herself at the back, so that she could admire the majestic mountain scenery through which they had to drive from the coast to reach Granada.

The bare grey mountains seemed almost deserted, and a cold wind whistled down the mountain passes. Caitlin could imagine what it must be like here in the winter when the mountains were covered with snow. Even now in summer they were a forbidding sight.

The coach dropped its passengers at the Alhambra gates, from where they walked into the beautiful palaces with their mosaic-decorated courts and fountains. It was getting very hot again, the sun pouring down on them, and the sound of cascading water was delightful. Caitlin and the other passengers followed the guide, listening to her lecture on the history and art of the Alhambra, but Caitlin preferred to use her eyes and just enjoy what she was seeing. She wished there were no other tourists thronging the palaces, and that she could sit down by the fountain with its beautifully carved lions and listen to the music of the water while she gazed at the exquisite blue mosaic on the roof and walls, the elaborate fretwork carving of creamy stone.

But she had been warned not to get left behind, and other parties of tourists from coaches were surging on their heels, so she had to follow her guide and the other passengers on through the crowded palace.

After that, they spent an hour strolling through the beautiful gardens surrounding the palace. It was easy to imagine what an effect the Alhambra had had on the minds of visitors when it was built, in medieval times. There could have been nothing like it in Christian Europe; no great airy palace full of arches and courts, with stone water channels running everywhere, making it possible to fill the rooms and gardens with fountains, no terraces of gardens which bloomed with roses even in the brutal heat of the Spanish summer.

She tired, in the end, and sat down on a bench under a tree to wait for the rest of the party, gazing dreamily along the gravel paths at the towering trees, the massed roses and lilies around which heavy-bodied bees hummed and sang. At a distance, she saw a bald head, and frowned. Surely that wasn't the man from the plane again?

An alarming thought struck her. What if he was following her? What if he was one of Monro's detectives? Her heart missed a beat. If he was, then Monro had already found her, would know by now where she was—might even be waiting for her in Málaga.

'Are we all here now?' asked the guide from the coach, and there was a chorus of assent. The woman counted them all. 'Now, you must be hungry. We go to lunch.'

Caitlin glanced back over her shoulder nervously as they walked out of the gardens, but there was no sign of the bald man. With relief she decided that he was just a tourist, like herself. No doubt everyone who came to this coast visited the Alhambra.

The guide took them on to lunch in a typical Andalucían restaurant. Caitlin wasn't hungry and ate little of the garlic and tomato soup, followed by a very bony grilled fish, followed by a casserole of meat and vegetables, but she ate the local ice-cream because she was very hot and needed to cool down.

On the coach drive back to Málaga she slept fitfully, her head nodding against the back of the seat, and dreamt of cool colonnades in which fountains sent glittering sprays of water into the air; dreamt of Monro walking through the courts of the Alhambra, his dark figure glimpsed here and there among the marble columns, appearing, then vanishing.

She woke up with a start when they stopped outside her hotel and the driver called her name. Flushed and almost feverish, she left the coach and went up to her room to take a cool shower and rest before dinner. Turning under the shower jet, her eyes closed as the refreshing water hit her overheated body and ran slowly down over her head, shoulders, breasts, belly, hips and legs, she thought about those dreams and felt her heart turn over as she finally admitted how deeply she felt about Monro.

She hadn't been in love in the beginning. In fact, she had disliked him at first sight. She had been hostile for a long time; angered by his arrogance and insistence on his own way, by his methods in getting what he wanted, by the insolence with which he had sent his secretary to get her for him.

Her first view of him, though, had been distorted, partly because she had still been bitter over her treatment by Roddy, partly by Monro's own behaviour. She had gradually got to know him over the past two years as his wife. He was a loving, caring father. He was a sensual and passionate lover. He was a clever, shrewd businessman. Monro was a lot of different things. He had a great many different facets to his nature. He wasn't easy to understand. What complex man ever was? She knew she didn't yet understand him, but underneath her surface hostility to him, underneath her coldness, her wariness and distance from him, there was another feeling hidden.

She didn't know if it was love. It was a very powerful emotion, whatever it was; it was eating away inside her like acid, and she didn't know how to cope with the pain of it. It was a muddled emotion, too, compounded of anger, resentment, outrage and a sensual passion.

She missed him; she ached to feel his mouth, to touch him and feel him touching her. She longed to hear his voice, look at him. At the same time, she wished he were there so that she could yell at him, release her rage and the hurt deep inside her. She wanted to hit him, her hands clenched, but she knew that, though she might begin by slapping him, she would end by touching him in a very different way, because she was dying to make love to him.

She lay down on her bed, wrapped in a towelling robe, and slowly fell asleep.

The next day, she caught a coach to Marbella, and booked into the Hotel Puente Romano, a hotel surrounded by a simply designed complex of whitewashed, adobe-style apartments set among luxuriant tropical gardens with a genuine

Roman bridge set among them. Caitlin was given a suite on the second floor of an apartment block right next to one of the swimming-pools which were scattered throughout the gardens. She had a bedroom, bathroom, sitting-room, all spacious, with comfortable furniture. A balcony led off the sitting-room. The hotel manager showed her to her suite, opening the white shutters so that sunlight flooded the rooms. He threw the french windows open, too, and when he had gone she went out on to the balcony to admire the view of the pool outside, the fringe of palm trees, and beyond them, not far away, the blue sea.

There were a few people in the pool, swimming and splashing about. There were others strolling along the winding paths, beside the little stream, crossing the bridges, exploring the tropical gardens. Among them was a security man who looked up sharply at her, spoke into a walkie-talkie he carried, then walked on.

Security was tight, here, she had been told. Night and day, there was a uniformed security officer walking the paths between the apartments, keeping an eye on guests and making sure that no intruders got in.

She felt safe here, and very peaceful. She sat down on the whitewashed concrete seat which ran along the low wall edging the tile-floored balcony. There was a table out there, too, so that you could eat meals in your own apartment, either cooking them yourself in the tiny cupboard-hidden kitchen, or sending for them from the hotel restaurant.

Somehow she felt sure Monro would not find her here. She had hidden her trail by taking a coach. She could relax now and enoy a holiday, sunbathing, swimming, resting, while she worked out what she would do next.

She had to get a job, and some time soon she would ring Joe at home and ask him for help to find work. First, though, she would give Monro time to read her letter and realise that they had never really been married, that, in fact, she was still legally Roddy's wife, and it would take years for her to free herself, because she could be sure of one thing—Roddy wouldn't make it easy for her. He wouldn't just give her a divorce. He would want her to pay through the nose, for one!

She spent the next few days inside the hotel grounds. It seemed safer. She always got up early and swam in the pool outside the apartment block, went back to her suite, showered, dressed and walked through the grounds for breakfast at the hotel. At a leisurely pace she then wandered down to the beach, admiring the gardens as she walked. She lay on a lounger under a straw umbrella until lunchtime. The hotel was famous for its cold and hot buffet lunch. The buffet tables groaned with food, from caviare and smoked salmon to steak or lobster, from avocado pear piled with crab and pineapple in a creamy sauce to raw vegetables served julienne-style, in thin strips, which you ate with a dip of some kind. Caitlin ate lightly at a table by herself, fending off advances from any of the male guests who happened to be there alone, then she went to her suite to spend her siesta hours on her bed, wearing only a thin cotton robe, with the windows open but the shutters closed against the hot sun.

She usually slept and woke to find the room filled with bluish shadows as the air cooled a little with the end of the day. Outside in the gardens birds called and people splashed in the pool. Caitlin liked to lie there listening to the drowsy sounds before getting up to go and shower again before dinner, which she also ate in the hotel. She usually had a half-bottle of wine with her meal. The wine was soporific and made sure she would sleep.

The days slid past like that—tranquil, except when unwelcome thoughts intruded on the peace. On the Friday morning at eleven she thought about Roddy waiting for her in the Food Hall at Harrods, and bit her lip, wishing she knew what he would do when he realised she hadn't come. Monro must have received her letter by now, surely? He would know all about it. If Roddy rang, he would find he had bitten off more than he had bargained for. What would Monro do to him?

She was glad she wasn't there to find out. Angry, Monro was very dangerous, and after reading her letter he was going to be angry. Roddy deserved what would happen to him. She felt no sympathy for Roddy. She only hoped Monro didn't actually kill him. If Roddy tried to blackmail him, that was certainly a possibility. Monro was not the man to stand still for being blackmailed.

She was beginning to be edgy now, wondering what was happening back in England. That evening, she decided to ring Joe. He might know something, and she could trust him.

'Darling, where are you?' Joe asked, and she told him because by now Monro wasn't going to come looking for her.

'Marbella?' Joe said, and laughed a lot. 'What on earth are you doing there?'

'Tourist things. Sun, sea and sand, and very restful it is, too.'

'No need to sound so defiant! I like Spain,' Joe said. 'Darling, I have had *visits*.'

She groaned. 'Monro?'

'And one of his henchmen, a nasty character who seemed to think he was acting in a Humphrey Bogart film. He kept blowing smoke in my face and talking about accidents I could have.'

She was appalled. 'Joe! How dreadful! I'm so sorry. I can't believe Monro would threaten you like that.'

'He didn't get where he is by being Mr Nice Guy.'

'Even so! What did he say, Joe, when he came himself?'

'He seemed to think I knew where you were. He told me he was having me watched. I told him I hoped his Peeping Toms had a good time.' He laughed, but he was clearly very angry. 'We had a row, came close to killing each other, and he slammed off.' Joe paused. 'Do I take it that you aren't going back to him?'

'No,' she said tersely. 'Joe, did he say anything else? Mention anybody?'

'Who would he mention?' There was a little silence, then Joe said, 'Is there somebody else, Caitlin? Did you elope with someone?'

'No, nothing like that. There's nobody else. It's just that...' Her voice trailed off. 'Joe, could you discreetly look around for work for me? London, or New York? I know modelling is out now, but there must be plenty of jobs I could do around the fashion world. Could you keep your eyes and ears open for me?'

'Sure. I'll ask around. I'm sure I can find you something. Give me your number there, and I'll be in touch.'

She told him where she was staying and he whistled. 'I've heard of it, never been there. Is it nice?'

'Fabulous.' She told him about the tropical gardens, the blue sea, the pools and whispering palms.

'Stop, you're making me green with envy!' he groaned. 'You know, that would be perfect for a fashion show I'm thinking of putting on for a charity, international affair, you know the kind. I must take a look at the Puente Romano some day.'

She rang off and curled up on her bed, wondering if Roddy had been in touch with Monro yet, or whether he was still trying to get hold of her. Sooner or later he was bound to realise she had run away, and he would then ring Monro. She was sure of that. Roddy needed the money for that debt of his. Gambling? she thought scornfully, then frowned, as a totally new idea hit her. Drugs?

Knowing Roddy as she did, she thought it could be either.

She was eating her lunch the following day when a familiar figure strolled towards her and her eyes opened wide in surprise. 'Joe!'

He dropped into the chair opposite. 'Hi, sweetheart! You're getting quite a nice tan.'

'What on earth are you doing here?' She went pale, looking past him. 'Joe, you haven't told——'

'Monro? What do you take me for? Of course not. I decided to spend the weekend in the sun, that's all. I flew in early this morning to Gibraltar and drove across the border.'

She gave him a wary look. What was in his mind, though, flying over here to join her? He was wearing an elegant biscuit linen suit with a warm tan sports shirt, and looked very Latin. She had always known that Joe liked her, but she had never felt uneasy with him before. She hoped she was not going to have to slap him down. She didn't want to lose one of her best friends.

Glancing at her salad and cold chicken, he said, 'I think I'll join you in some of that. Is the food good here?'

'Terrific,' she said. 'Go up to the buffet table and see the incredible variety of dishes on offer!'

Joe wandered over there and came back with a piled plate, grinning. 'I can see I'm going to like it here. What is there to do at night?' He gave her a wicked look. 'Apart from the obvious, that is!'

She made a face. She hoped he wasn't going to make sex jokes very often. He never had before—why was he doing it now? 'They have a cabaret in the bar some nights, and there is dancing other times, but I always go to bed early. I eat early, just a light meal, then take a stroll through the gardens before bed. I'm trying to get lots of sleep.'

'Sounds too, too exciting!' mocked Joe. 'Well, now I'm here maybe we can think of something to do.'

That afternoon, however, Caitlin kept to her established routine and went to bed for a siesta. They met for dinner, though, and danced afterwards for an hour to a very good Spanish band. Then Caitlin went to bed.

'Spoil-sport!' complained Joe, but she smilingly told him it wouldn't do him any harm to take some rest for a couple of days.

In the morning, though, he was not at breakfast, and when he did surface, just before lunch in the bar, she gathered that he had been up very late the previous night, drinking with people he had met in the bar.

They went into lunch, and as they ate they talked about various jobs he suggested. None of them was very exciting, but, as Joe pointed out, she had no training for anything but modelling.

'Unless...' he began, as they were walking back across the gardens to the apartment blocks, and she pricked up her ears.

'Unless what?'

'Well, you could start training as a sales-woman in a fashion house.'

'Yes,' she agreed, nodding. 'If I could get a job with a good house.'

'I'd give you a start,' Joe said offhandedly, and she gave him a quick look, feeling rather guilty because she had practically asked him for this offer of a job. What else could he have done, in the circumstances?

'Joe! Would you?' She flung her arms around him and hugged him. 'Oh, you're such a darling!'

Joe held her waist, smiling down at her. 'I shall expect you to work like mad, mind you. And I'm not easy to work for, I'm told.'

'I know,' she said ironically.

'Some people have called me a power-maniac.'

'I know.'

'I do lose my temper now and then.'

'I know.'

'But I do try to be fair, and I'll always cool down after I've lost my temper, and you won't get a better training as a *vendeuse* with any other house in London.'

'I know,' she said, and smiled affectionately at him, her eyes full of gratitude. 'I'll work like crazy, Joe, and you won't regret giving me this chance.'

'I hope not,' he said sternly. 'Now, go and have your siesta and I'll take a wander around the place. I'm going to check it out to see if it would suit for this charity fashion show. I was going to focus on beach wear anyway, and this would be the perfect background for that. See you later.'

She turned down a winding path between exotic flowers and palm trees, and climbed the steps to her apartment block, beginning to feel drowsy now. She had got used to taking a siesta after lunch when it was really too hot to move.

Her suite was always cool and shadowy in the afternoon because she had left the shutters closed during lunch. She let herself in, yawning, and went straight into the bathroom. After washing, she took off her chic cream dress, and slipped into the cotton wrap she always wore for her siesta. Barefoot, she wandered out of the mirror-lined bathroom and then stopped dead, staring across the sitting-room at the french windows leading on to the balcony. They were open, and the shutters were ajar, allowing a beam of sunlight to fall across the room.

A dark shape loomed beyond the shutters. Her heart stopped. There was someone out on the balcony. A man. She stared intently, getting ready to run for the outer door, then the shutters were pushed wider and he walked back into the room, his face dark and hostile.

'Monro!' she whispered, clutching the lapels of her thin wrap. How had he found her? Had he had Joe followed? 'How . . . how did you get here?'

'Your lover led me here,' Monro bit out, his mouth cruel.

'He isn't my lover!'

'Don't lie to me!' There was violence in his eyes; he was as tense as a whiplash, and she fell silent under that dangerous stare. 'I might have been stupid enough to believe that once,' he grated, 'but I just saw you in his arms, and I won't be hoodwinked again!'

'You saw...' she faltered, her mind leaping ahead.

'Yes, I was out on that balcony, watching the two of you walking in the gardens. I saw you in his arms, so don't lie to me! I've had enough lies. You swore he wasn't your lover, yet I just saw you throw your arms round him and kiss him——'

'I didn't kiss him!'

His eyes glittered like black ice. 'I tell you I saw you! Don't try to convince me I've started seeing things that aren't there, because there's nothing wrong with my eyes.'

'I hugged him,' she insisted, and he snarled, his lip curling.

'A hug or a kiss—what difference does it make? You're here, and he flew over to join you as soon as he could—that is the truth of it.'

She couldn't argue about that. She was here—and Joe had flown over to join her. It wasn't the facts he had wrong—it was his interpretation of those facts. Joe was irrelevant, couldn't he see that? She looked at him uncertainly, puzzled that he hadn't mentioned Roddy.

'Didn't you get my letter?' she asked huskily, frowning.

He stiffened, staring at her. 'What letter?'

She didn't know what to say—clearly her letter
hadn't reached him yet. What on earth could have
happened to it? She had posted it days ago. It
ought to have been delivered the next morning,
or at the very least the day after that, but then
the English post lately had become more erratic
than ever before. If he hadn't read her letter he
did not know about Roddy, and presumably
Roddy had not yet approached him either.

'Well?' he grated, watching her face. 'What
did this letter say? That you were leaving me for
Fanucci, is that it? You can think again, Caitlin.
You aren't leaving me for anyone, least of all
some damned dressmaker. I told you the last time
I saw you . . . you are mine, and you'll stay mine
until I decide otherwise.' His eyes flashed down
over her with a savagery that made her flinch.

She pulled the neck of her wrap closer; it was
a flimsy protection, but it was all she had. 'I'm
not getting into another scene with you, Monro.
Will you please go?'

'Expecting someone?' His voice cut like a knife
and she began to tremble.

'No, of course not——'

'Fanucci, by any chance? Let me guess—he is
being a gentleman, taking a walk to give you a
chance to slip into something seductive? And any
minute now he'll be knocking on that door,
expecting to find you waiting for him with open
arms.'

She shook her head, her mouth dry with nerves
and fear. 'No, it isn't true, Monro. Joe isn't in
love with me, we aren't lovers——'

'Not yet?' His narrowed eyes probed her face like a scalpel in a wound, and she bit back a cry of terror at his expression. She had never really been afraid of Monro until that moment, but suddenly she was icy with fear.

'I swear we aren't,' she pleaded, and his face held a brooding menace.

'Well, he isn't going to have you now, either. When he comes to knock on the door, you will be otherwise engaged.'

She turned white, shaking. 'Monro...' She turned to run, too late. He took three steps and caught her, his hands cruel and remorseless, swept her up into his arms, and carried her into the bedroom.

CHAPTER SIX

CAITLIN couldn't bear to have Monro make love to her again as if they were deadly enemies, but she knew she couldn't physically stop him, so she fell back on woman's oldest weapon.

She began to cry, her hands over her face, the tears running down her cheeks. She wasn't acting. The tears were real. Her fear was real. Her pain was real.

Monro stood by the bed, holding her, and groaned angrily. 'Not that, please! Anything but tears! Why do women always have to resort to tears to get their own way? Stop it, Caitlin!'

She didn't stop crying, though, and at last he sat down on the bed with her still clutched in his arms, and rocked her like a child, her head cradled on his chest, his hand stroking her hair in a rough caress. 'Don't baby, don't,' he muttered, putting his cheek down against her hair. 'Shh...stop crying, there's a good girl.'

Her shuddering sobs died down and she stopped crying, leaning weakly against him and feeling safe in his arms.

'Better?' he whispered, and she nodded. Monro ran his fingers through her loose hair and then gripped a mass of it, pulling it back so that she had to look up at him.

'What were you crying over, anyway?' he asked sardonically, 'Yourself—or your boyfriend?'

She sat up, her face wet and her eyes still cloudy with tears, and pulled herself off his lap without him trying to stop her. 'Joe isn't my boyfriend, or my lover—Monro, why won't you listen?'

'I'll listen when you start telling me the truth!' he said drily.

'I wrote it to you,' she said huskily. 'In the letter...'

His black head tilted and his eyes narrowed. 'What exactly was in this letter?'

She took a deep breath. 'It's a long story.'

He pulled a chair over and straddled it, his legs on each side, his chin resting on the chair back. 'I've got all the time in the world.'

She sat on the edge of the bed, head bent, eyes lowered, her bare feet dangling towards the floor.

'I'll have to start at the beginning...my first marriage.'

'Ah, I was beginning to wonder when I would hear about that! I've even tried to dig out information on my own account, but I didn't find out much, and you always refused to talk about it.'

'I couldn't bear to remember. I was very young when I got married, and I picked the wrong man.' She saw his face change, his eyes flash.

'The wrong man? You mean, you didn't love your first husband?' His voice had a faint tremor in it.

'When I married him, yes, but...' She sighed. 'It didn't take long for me to learn to hate him. Roddy was vicious; he gambled, drank, had other women . . . and he could be violent. He had some very unpleasant friends, and tried to make me——' She broke off, closing her eyes, then plunged on huskily. 'He called it "being nice to them".'

Munro drew an unsteady breath. 'He did what? Caitlin . . .'

She risked a look at him, smiling crookedly. 'I refused, and he beat me up.' She said it in a shaky rush, and felt her words vibrating between them, saw Monro turn rigid, his mouth a white line. He picked up her hand and stared down at the slightness, the fragility of it.

'Did he hurt you badly?' he whispered, bending his head to touch his lips very gently to her wrist, where an agitated pulse beat.

'He was far too cunning to do that. If I'd been badly hurt someone might have found out. No, he just knocked me about, gave me some nasty-looking bruises, but it made no difference—I still wouldn't do what he wanted me to do. After that I hated him, and I was scared stiff of him by the time we moved into that hotel in Mexico City. The earthquake wasn't a tragedy for me, it was a blessed release. If it hadn't been for the earthquake, I would never have dared leave Roddy, because I would have been stranded out there, in a foreign country without any money and no way of getting back to England. I know you had the fixed idea that I was still in love with Roddy, but you couldn't have been more wrong.'

Monro was frowning, a darkness in his eyes. 'Why didn't you tell me all this two years ago?

Why did you let me go on thinking you were still mourning a dead man?'

She couldn't meet his eyes. 'I . . .'

His voice hardened, iced over again. 'You wanted to keep me at arm's length, and a myth about grieving for a dead husband was very useful?'

'No!' she protested angrily. 'I just couldn't, don't you see that? I didn't want to talk about it. It made me sick to remember, let alone talk about it, especially to you.'

His face took on an alert, watchful look. 'Why especially to me, Caitlin?'

'Because you asked me to marry you, and I couldn't bear you to know about my first marriage; it was all so sordid, so shameful——' Her voice broke, and Monro leant forward, his face gentle.

'None of it was your fault, Caitlin. You didn't have to feel ashamed.'

'But I did! It wasn't just that I couldn't tell you, Monro. I was actually terrified you might find out.'

'So that was why you kept refusing to see me, in the beginning?' he thought aloud, frowning. 'You must have been very wary of men.'

'You can say that again,' she agreed, laughing bitterly. 'My first marriage had been a disaster. Roddy taught me to be afraid of caring for anyone. I'd been in love with him, and I was badly mauled, so I was in no hurry to fall in love with anyone else.'

He put out a hand to touch her cheek, very lightly. 'Poor little Caitlin...and you were so young, too. Almost a child. My God, if I'd only known! Everything would have been different. I'd have realised what I was dealing with.'

'And you'd never have married me.'

'Oh, yes, you wouldn't have got away,' he said, his lips twisting in wry amusement. 'But I'd have handled you differently, been more careful with you. All this time I've thought that I was fighting the memory of a man you still loved even though he was dead.' She flinched, and he frowned, misunderstanding her expression. 'Now that it is out in the open...that you've talked to me about it...you must be on the way to forgetting, Caitlin! Aren't you?'

'I...' she began, and faltered, and his frown darkened.

'What else don't I know? And, anyway, what has this to do with why you ran away? Your first marriage doesn't explain why you've left me and come away with Joe Fanucci.'

She gave him a despairing look, ran her hands through her hair.

'Oh, please, Monro, leave Joe out of it. I promise you, he isn't involved...but Roddy is!'

He tensed, staring sharply. 'Roddy...*is*?'

Monro was clever; he had picked up her phrasing and the tone of her voice. He was watching her with those hard grey eyes, and already guessing what she was going to say, even though it seemed incredible.

'Yes,' she nodded, whispering as if afraid they might be overheard. 'He's...' The words wouldn't come, and she put out a hand which Monro took and held, instinctively rubbing it to inject some warmth into her frozen flesh. Caitlin's white lips parted then, and breathed the shocking truth. 'He...is alive.'

'Alive?' Monro repeated, pale and incredulous. 'Alive?' She nodded again, and he let out a long, harsh breath. 'My God!'

She bit her lip. 'I'm sorry. I'm sorry, Monro—it isn't easy for me to tell you this. That's why I wrote to you. I was afraid of telling you face to face. I know it was cowardly, but I couldn't face it.'

He stood up abruptly, paced the room, turned towards her, saying curtly, 'You lied to me? He didn't die in Mexico? But I saw the death certificate, I had a report from Mexico City on what happened... Are you telling me you cooked that up between you? He disappeared and you lied to the authorities?'

'No!' she denied, appalled by the accusation. 'I thought he was dead, too. How can you think I'd do such a thing?'

Monro groaned, came back towards her, his face contrite. 'I'm sorry, God knows what I'm saying...of course I know you wouldn't...'

'Why, it never even occurred to me that he might still be alive until I saw him the other night,' she said, and Monro came to a stop in front of her.

'Saw him? You've seen him recently? Where?'
Then his eyes pierced her face and he took a long,
deep breath. 'At the art gallery—when you
fainted? That night I knew something was very
wrong!'

'I made it obvious by fainting, I suppose,' she
said wearily. 'I couldn't help myself—I had just
seen Roddy—he was working as one of the
waiters, he gave you a drink.'

Monro's face was grim. 'He was that close? If
I'd had any idea, I'd have...'

She was barely aware of his reaction, herself
shuddering at the memory of that terrible
moment of shock. 'I stared, I couldn't believe
my eyes, then he looked at me and there was that
expression on his face... I recognised it and felt
sick. Mockery, cruelty...it isn't easy to pin it
down, but it was never a pleasant look. It meant
that Roddy was about to do something vicious.'

'Bastard!' muttered Monro, watching her and
taut with anger. 'What did he do to you? Tell
me. I want to know it all now. What did the
bastard do to you?'

'I can't...' She averted her face, shivering.
'That night I just went icy cold and the room
started going round and round, then I fainted.'

'Why didn't you tell me then?' Monro grated
out, his brow black. 'While he was there and I
could tackle him?'

'I couldn't! When I came to, Jeffrey was there,
listening, and then I started wondering if I had
imagined it, if it had really been Roddy. He
hadn't said anything to me. It might have been

someone who looked like him. I wasn't sure what
to do, but I was scared of telling you anything.
I decided to get a private detective to investigate
the waiters who had been there that night.'

'And he found Roddy?'

'No,' she said flatly. 'I didn't need to engage
a detective—Roddy rang me.'

Monro gave an exclamation. 'Of course! The
mysterious phone-call!'

'Yes. Roddy told me to meet him and then rang
off, so you see why I had to go out.'

'No, it was stupid!' he bit out. 'You should
have told me and let me deal with it! There was
no need for you to take orders from him!'

'But I had to talk to him, to find out what had
happened...I didn't know what to do. I was still
taking it in—all the implications of Roddy being
alive.'

His mouth grim, Monro nodded. 'I can
understand that. I'm in the same boat now. I'm
beginning to realise what a problem we have...'

She gave him a brief, miserable look. 'I wondered when it would dawn on you.'

He grimaced. 'Well, go on...so you met him?
What in God's name did he have to say for
himself?'

'He told me why he wasn't in the hotel when
the earthquake started. He had picked up
another woman and gone home with her.'

Monro's brows met above his angry eyes. 'So
he was that sort of swine, was he? Had it happened before? Did you know about his affairs?'

'That was typical,' she said with a tired indifference. 'I just thought he was in the bar drinking, that evening. He was always going off with other women, though.'

Monro was watching her with bitter intensity. 'I've never understood what women saw in men like that, but I suppose you were too young to know what you were doing. Well, after the earthquake, why didn't he come back? Why——?'

'When he realised that he was supposed to be dead, he thought it was a great joke. He decided to take advantage of it. I think he owed people a lot of money and being dead was one way of getting out of all his debts. People did ask me for the money, but I didn't have any, and so they gave up. There was insurance money, but it was a pitiful amount, and the company wouldn't pay anyway. They said they would pay in three years; they claimed they had to wait that long. In the end, I just forgot about it. They were a South American firm.'

'They knew you were left penniless, a child of eighteen, and they didn't care?' Monro's rage burnt in his eyes, darkening them.

She shrugged. 'What did it matter to them?'

Monro's jaw clenched. 'Or to your swine of a husband, apparently?'

'No, that was the other big advantage to him—he got rid of me as well as all his creditors. He had been bored with me for ages, he said. I was just a nuisance.'

Monro's hands clenched into fists. 'He said that to you? If he were here now, I'd kill him!'

He walked across the room and back, his body moving tensely, in the prowl of a restless tiger. 'Did he realise you had married again? Oh, yes, of course, he must have known, to get your telephone number.'

'Oh, he knew!' She laughed shortly. 'That was why he wanted to see me. He was prepared to stay dead, at a price.'

'Ah!' Monro stood still, staring down into her eyes. 'Blackmail?'

She nodded, feeling ashamed, as though by marrying Roddy in the first place she were responsible for him and everything he did. Roddy felt no shame, no guilt—but then it was bred into women to feel both even when they were absolutely innocent.

'He took my earrings,' she whispered.

'Earrings?' Monro repeated blankly, looking at her ears, reaching out to touch the one that had been hurt, his fingertip gentle. 'I remember—your ear was bleeding...' His face tightened a second later. 'You said a mugger had snatched your sapphire earrings.'

'Roddy was the mugger.'

'He snatched your earrings and made your ear bleed?' Monro's jaw hardened. 'Everything you tell me about him makes me wonder what on earth you saw in him in the first place! How could you have loved a man like that?'

'I was very young.'

'And very stupid, obviously,' Monro said shortly.

'Yes, I must have been, but Roddy educated me.' She laughed angrily. 'I wasn't that young and that stupid after six months with him. The lessons he taught me went deep, too. I couldn't trust another man for years. I didn't feel I could trust anyone, come to that. I no longer had any faith in my own judgement. I distrusted emotions, I preferred to use my head rather than my heart.'

Monro eyed her sideways, his profile sardonic, but all he said was, 'So he snatched your earrings—but they were only trinkets, not worth more than a few hundred. That can't have been all he wanted!'

'No, he wanted money—lots of it. He suggested I sold some more of my jewellery, to pay him off, if I didn't want you to know we weren't legally married after all. He had a lot of fun pointing out how much the newspapers would love the story. I knew you'd hate it. I knew you would be so embarrassed. All your friends reading about it——'

'How much did he want?' Monro was even angrier now, and he frightened her.

Huskily, she told him.

'Twenty thousand?' Monro laughed, his grey eyes glittering. 'Only twenty? Peanuts. He must have a pretty shrewd idea how much I'm worth, and that twenty thousand would be petty cash to me. No, that was a first bite, just to test the water. If you had paid, he would have been back for more.'

'I worked that out for myself,' she said flatly. 'That's why I ran. He had given me until yesterday to find the money. I decided that the only thing I could do was go away. I wrote to you, explaining, setting the record straight, so that you could deal with the matter in whatever way you chose. If I wasn't around, it seemed to me it would be easier for you to deal with it. I suspected that if I didn't show up with the money Roddy would try to blackmail you instead, and then you could bring the police in. After all, you didn't know I was married, you didn't knowingly commit bigamy.'

'Neither did you,' Monro said curtly, watching her. 'Or so you say!'

'I didn't know!' she insisted. 'If I'd had any idea at all, I would have divorced him years ago. I thought I was free, though. It never even occurred to me that he might not be dead.'

'Have you got a telephone number for him? An address?'

She shook her head. 'I was to meet him in the Food Hall at Harrods. I met him there the first time he rang, the morning I went out after fainting, when he snatched my earrings. We met in Harrods and then took a taxi to Kensington Gardens and walked around, where nobody could hear what we were saying. I think he wanted to be sure I wasn't being followed, because he kept looking around as if he was nervous. He certainly didn't want me to know where he could be found.'

Monro paced up and down again, frowning. 'Describe him.'

She shivered. 'I'd rather not.'

'I have to know what he looks like!' he said roughly.

He was talking to her as if he hated her again. She looked away, her eyes stinging with tears, swallowed the bitter taste in her mouth, and began a slow, reluctant description of Roddy.

'He should be easy to find, if he's really as sexy as you seem to think he is!' Monro muttered, moving to the door.

'Sexy? I hate him!' she said, and Monro gave her a quick sideways look.

'You have good reason to! But you can stop worrying. I'll deal with him for you, you can bet on that!'

'Don't go looking for him!' she burst out, and he scowled.

'I thought you hated him. Why are you trying to protect him?'

'I'm not! Just listen. Let Roddy find you! He will, when he can't get in touch with me. He needs the money, remember. He'll have to get it from you if I'm out of reach. He'll try to blackmail you, then you can get the police to deal with him, without needing to get involved with him yourself!'

'You stay here and relax, forget about the whole thing! I'll sort this out,' said Monro gently, brushing a stray lock of hair back from her pale face. 'Try to calm down, Caitlin. You'll make yourself ill if you don't stop fretting. You live on your nerves too much. You can trust me to cope with this problem for you.' He smiled at her, his eyes warm, then turned and a second later was gone.

She ran after him, anxiety in her face, but he was already out of sight, so she went back into her suite, out on to the balcony to see if she could catch a glimpse of him in the gardens, but the only person she could see was Joe, who was taking snapshots of some ducks on a pond.

She looked at him wryly. Monro had shown signs of jealousy of Joe, but that didn't mean he loved her, only that he regarded her as his exclusive property and disliked the idea of anyone else near her. Well, at least she wouldn't have to patch Joe up after a violent encounter with Monro—which poor Joe would undoubtedly have lost—or apologise to him for the totally false ideas Monro seemed to have about their relationship!

She went back into her bedroom, closing the shutters behind her, plunging the room into cool shadow again, and lay down on the bed, but she didn't sleep. She wished she knew what Monro was really planning. She didn't care a fig what happened to Roddy—her only concern was for Monro. If he half killed Roddy, he might find himself in serious trouble with the law, and that would make the eventual Press coverage all the more excited. It would all make such a great gossip story! She knew how the British Press loved to hound anyone with a famous name who had been foolish enough to make a mistake, and this particular piece of gossip had so many fascinating angles to it. The high and mighty tumbling from their pedestals always made the headlines, but when you added a resurrection, sex, a charge of bigamy, blackmail and violence the story might run for weeks.

She drifted off into a light doze eventually, then woke up with a start hearing voices out in the garden. For a moment she was disorientated and couldn't remember where she was, then she sat up, yawning, and decided to take a shower.

When she wandered back into the sitting room, wrapped in a huge white bath sheet, the air seemed stuffy so she opened the shutters and let in the late afternoon sunlight. A lethargy had overcome her. She had been running for what seemed an age, afraid of Roddy's threats, afraid of Monro finding out that they weren't really married—and now it was all out in the open and she had faced up to the fact that her marriage was finished, and to her surprise instead of being miserable she was full of relief.

The strain had been lifted. She could relax. So she took her time in getting dressed, choosing a light, floating, gauzy dress, blue and lavender Indian muslin, which Joe had designed for her and which she knew was one of his own favourites. The dress suited her mood.

She and Joe met in the hotel bar half an hour before dinner. A well-known pop star was sitting at the piano, playing Cole Porter melodies, for his own pleasure and that of a party of his friends who happened to be staying there with him in his own private suite in the hotel. Joe knew several of the women, who were customers of his, and who came over to kiss him and be introduced to Caitlin. They gave her quick, assessing, speculative looks, hearing her name, or perhaps even recognising her before Joe told them who she was, and she could read their minds like books. They were wondering if she and Joe were having an affair; they were wondering if her wealthy husband knew she was there!

'I shan't be sorry to get out of this goldfish bowl,' she said to Joe, who gave her a wry smile.

'They can be cats! Ignore them.' He looked down into his cocktail, twiddling the little gold umbrella the bar staff had put into the drink.

'Caitlin, it might get back to your husband— that you were seen here with me. Had you thought of that? How will that affect whatever action you plan to take?'

'Divorce?' She shook her head. 'No, don't worry about that aspect, Joe.' There wouldn't be a divorce, but she wasn't ready to explain that to Joe, or anyone else, yet.

He frowned. 'You might not plan on having a divorce, but your husband might have other ideas. If he found out I was here with you——'

'He already knows.'

Joe did a double-take. 'He knows? You told him?'

'He saw you this afternoon.'

'He's here?' Joe glanced around the bar. 'When did he get here? I thought you hadn't told him where you were.'

'I hadn't.' She looked wryly at him, and Joe stared back briefly, then gave a groan, raking a hand through his hair.

'Don't tell me he followed me here?'

She nodded. 'I'm afraid so.'

'I led him to you! Caitlin, I'm sorry—what on earth can I say? I could kick myself. I hope he didn't make things too difficult.' He paused, frowning, obviously at a loss to know what to say. 'Caitlin...tell me if he turns really nasty, won't you? You don't have to put up with that sort of thing, you know. I've had a taste of his methods now—that guy he sent to put the fear of God into me, for instance! I know that wasn't Ritchie himself, but he employed that fellow. If he so much as touches you, just yell for me, OK?'

'He won't hurt me, Joe,' she said, hoping to sound convincing, but ever since they had met up in here she had been unconsciously looking over her shoulder, wondering if Monro had left anyone to watch them, or even if Monro himself might still be at the hotel. He hadn't actually said he was going home, had he? She had just formed that impression, and, in spite of her firm denials to Joe, she was nervous of Monro.

'He wasn't very happy about seeing you here with me, though,' she said, slightly mischievously. 'But I don't think he'll actually try to kill you, so there's no need to panic.'

'Well, that's a relief!' Joe said sarcastically.

He drank the rest of his cocktail in one swallow. 'So where is he? Will he be having dinner with us? Should I go and change into my suit of armour?'

'I think he has gone back to London now. He flew over here in his private jet.'

'His private jet? But of course!' Joe gave her a comic look and she laughed. 'Nice to be that rich,' he added. 'So much you can buy yourself,' and he flicked another teasing look at Caitlin. 'If I were a multimillionaire . . .'

'Aren't you?' she mocked in turn, and he grinned.

'I wish I were. Caitlin, why has he gone back so soon? Hardly seems worth the trip. Did he fly over for afternoon tea, or something? He missed lunch, now he's going to miss dinner.'

She looked at her watch. 'Talking of dinner, isn't it time we went into the restaurant?'

Joe pulled an amused face, recognising that she had deliberately changed the subject, but he didn't argue.

They took their time over dinner, and walked back through the floodlit gardens together, listening to frogs croaking in the stream. Joe glanced up at her balcony, his face rueful. 'I suppose I'm going to have to say goodnight.'

She took his meaning and smiled. 'Yes, Joe. Sorry.'

'I didn't rush over here with the idea of climbing into bed with you, darling, but it does occur to me that it would be fun. No strings, no commitments . . . just fun.' He raised one brow.

She shook her head. 'Sorry, not my idea of fun, I'm afraid.'

'And you're stupid enough to be in love with your own husband?' Joe had a wry look as he watched her flush and look away. 'I wouldn't have come if I hadn't believed you meant it when you said your marriage was over, and I don't just mean that I was being an opportunist swine and hurrying over to see what I could get out of the situation. I thought you might need a shoulder to cry on—but I can see you don't, so I'll be flying back to London myself tomorrow morning. At least I've come to a decision about this place—it will be perfect for my charity show if I can get the right terms.'

'Well, I hope you do—it should be a great setting for a fashion show.'

'With any luck you'll be working for me then, if you still want the job.'

'I do! I'm really looking forward to starting. I'll be coming back to London myself in a few days. I'll be in touch—and Joe, thank you for coming,' she said, smiling at him gently. 'I was feeling lonely and I appreciated the company.'

'Oh, forget it,' he said, kissed her quickly on the cheek, and walked away into the night.

She did not see him at breakfast the next morning, and felt a little melancholy as she strolled down to the beach to sunbathe under one of the straw umbrellas. She read and listened to music on her headphones for several hours, then walked back to the apartment block, meaning to have a shower. The pool was empty, though, and she suddenly decided to take a swim, while she

could be certain of being alone, so she changed
into a black bikini and went down to the pool.

The water was cool and refreshing. She swam
lazily, her eyes half shut against the glare of the
sun, meaning only to stay for a few minutes, then
suddenly she heard a splash as someone else dived
into the pool. She glanced round and saw
someone swimming towards her, cutting
smoothly through the water, the gleam of the
sunlight on brown arms and powerful shoulders.

She couldn't see very clearly in that glaring sun,
so she put a hand up to shade her eyes. In the
dazzle of the Spanish light she just made out a
wet, seal-like head. It couldn't be Joe's dark
head. He had gone hours ago. But whoever it
was was coming straight for her, and a peculiar
panic surged into her.

She began to swim urgently towards the tiled
side of the pool, but as she got there and started
to climb out she felt hands grab her ankles and
drag her backwards, her long, wet blonde hair
blinding her as it was whipped across her face.

She struggled helplessly, and was drawn downwards, downwards, into the water, coughing and
spluttering, utterly panic-stricken. He was trying
to drown her!

CHAPTER SEVEN

His body twisted upwards around Caitlin's, his arms sliding along her back to enclose her and pull her so close to him that they were face to face, their hair streaming together like some strange seaweed, his black, hers silvery in the water. She clutched his wet body and his mouth caught hers as they broke back to the surface into the sunlight.

He lifted his head, still clasping her and, gasping for breath, Caitlin stared into his grey eyes. 'I thought you were trying to drown me!' She had to stop to cough, leaning on him, her face on his naked brown chest. When she could speak again she said huskily, 'Have you been back to England? Has . . . anything happened?' She couldn't bring herself to use Roddy's name, but she was on tenterhooks to know if he had been in touch, if Monro had done anything about him.

'I've been to London, and back, and I've dealt with your first husband, don't worry.'

'Dealt with him?' Her heart constricted. 'How?'

'He's gone,' Monro coolly told her, then his legs entwined with hers and he pulled her back down into the pool.

Caitlin was exploding with questions, but she couldn't free herself. She was drawn through the water with him, their bodies corkscrewing, over and over, arms around each other. Monro kissed her again, his hands wandering casually, until at last they had to emerge again, for air.

That time Caitlin broke free and swam hurriedly to the side to climb out. Monro followed her. Streaming with water, she picked up her towelling robe from the lounger on to which she had flung it before she had got into the pool, and Monro walked over, tanned and long-legged, to get a towel from the lounger next to hers.

She put on her robe and tied the belt at the waist, flicked her long, wet hair forwards, bending so that it hung in front of her face like a curtain, seized it in both hands and wrung it out, then flicked it back behind her again, straightening.

Monro watched her, towelling himself in a leisurely way. 'Shall we talk here or go inside?'

She was afraid of being interrupted, of eavesdroppers. 'I think we'd better go inside.'

In her suite, Monro coolly picked up the phone and dialled room service to order drinks. Caitlin wandered out on to her balcony and sat down, leaning back against the parapet, her knees up and her arms clasped around them. A pine tree grew close to the apartment block, giving the warm air a fresh, pungent scent and leaving blocks of dark blue shadow on the white walls. A wood dove sat in it, giving its familiar crooning call, preening its feathers. Everything around her was so peaceful, so beautiful, and she was on the edge of panic, her heart beating too fast, her mind rapping out staccato questions.

Monro came out on to the balcony, his brown body still bare except for the brief black silk trunks. She looked at his body and her mouth went dry. She looked away, at the pine tree cradling its dove.

'Tell me what happened...' she whispered.

'He had been ringing on and off for a day or so, I gathered, when I got back. He wasn't leaving any name, but Austell was sure it was always the same man.'

She groaned, closing her eyes. 'Austell...' The thought of the butler knowing anything about this made her feel sick.

'Austell has no idea what's going on,' Monro said. 'I've told him that you are over here, he knows I've joined you for a holiday, that's all. Of course, he connected your first husband's calls with you, because Austell has good hearing and a first-class memory. He knew that this man who kept ringing me had been trying to get in touch with you, at first, and he discreetly let me know as much. I told him to put this man through to me the next time he rang, and sure enough Roddy rang a couple of hours later, and Austell put him through to me.'

She swallowed. 'He asked you for the money?'

'Not over the phone. He's far too shrewd for that. He knows all about the various devices for recording phone-calls. No, he just said he had some information about you that he thought I should hear, and he insisted that we met in Piccadilly. He told me to stand still on the pavement near the bus-stop, as if I was waiting for the tourist bus, and he would find me. I said I'd be there, but I had already set some wheels in motion before I left here.'

'What wheels?' she asked, frowning. 'Monro.... you didn't go to the police? But——'

'Not the police,' he said. 'I didn't think the police could handle what I wanted. No, I got in touch with a detective agency I've used many times before; in fact they investigated you and your first husband before I married you.'

'I remember,' she said flatly, still frowning.

'I know it annoyed you,' Monro said, a few inches away and watching her intently. 'But I have to protect myself—maybe now you can understand why. Anyway, I asked them to check your first husband out again—more thoroughly this time. When they ran the original check on him, they didn't go back beyond his marriage to you. This time, I told them to go right back to his day of birth. I told them to dig out everything they could, however vague, and to move fast. An hour before I was due to meet up with him in Piccadilly they came through with a first report, and handed me the weapon I needed.'

'Weapon?' she repeated in stupefaction, putting her feet down and standing up because she couldn't just sit there listening any more. She was too agitated. She had to move about.

'Oh, not a gun or a knife!' he said, smiling coldly. 'Just a fact. Cold facts can be more deadly than a gun, sometimes. When I met Roddy Butler, I hit him with that fact and he ran out of our lives for good.'

Caitlin was bewildered; she walked to and fro, across the cold stone floor of the balcony. 'What fact, though? Stop talking in riddles and explain what you mean! What did you find out?'

'You weren't the one who committed bigamy, he was!' Monro said, and she stopped dead, staring, her blue eyes enormous.

'He——?'

'Was already married when he met you. He had dumped his previous wife several years earlier, and she had been looking for him ever since, to pay for the support of their child——'

'Child?'

'A little girl, now aged twelve. His wife eventually divorced him in his absence, and has remarried, but that divorce didn't take place until after he married you.'

'After he married me?' For a moment she couldn't take in what he was saying, the shock of these new revelations had stunned her. 'Then that means——'

'You were never his wife,' Monro agreed coolly.

She sat down abruptly, her legs suddenly weak beneath her, and stared at the pine tree and the blue sky behind it, with the paler blue of the sea reaching out to the far horizon, while very slowly it sank in—she had never been Roddy's legal wife!

'But are you sure? What did he say?'

There was a ring at the doorbell of her suite, and Monro called out to the room-service waiter to come in. He appeared, bowed to them, placed their drinks in front of them on the table on the balcony, and discreetly vanished again.

Monro picked up his glass and tilted it towards her in a graceful silent toast. She picked up her own glass and drank. Her mouth felt as if it were full of ashes. She was dying of thirst. Monro drank half his whisky, watching her over the rim of the glass, and she was nervously aware of the way he watched her. A disturbing ache began in the pit of her stomach and she swallowed some more of the Martini he had ordered for her.

'You were going to tell me what Roddy said...' she prompted huskily.

'Yes,' Monro said, in an oddly abstracted tone, his grey eyes narrowed and gleaming as they stared back at her. 'Yes, well, he started out by denying it, of course, as one might have expected of someone of his type, but when I said I was going to pass on his current whereabouts to his wife, so that she could sue him for maintenance for his child, as well as contacting the police to make a complaint against him, he finally admitted the truth and we made a deal.'

'What sort of deal?' she asked anxiously.

Monro grimaced. 'I'm not too happy about what we agreed on—I don't like letting that bastard get away with it all. I'd have liked to see him go to prison for a stiff sentence, and be forced to pay his real wife every penny he possessed—but if he had to stand trial, so would we.

Your name would be dragged into court and plastered all over every newspaper in the country. I knew you'd hate it, and, from my own angle, I'd hate it too.'

'It could be very unfortunate for your company shares,' she agreed, a sick relief seeping through her. If Roddy had really gone away, and this time for good, she would be able to sleep at night again.

Monro gave her a dry look. 'There's that, too. It seems unfair, but, in this situation, if he is punished for what he did then so are we, although we are the innocent parties! So after I'd thought about it for a while I decided to let Roddy go, with the proviso that if he showed up anywhere near either of us again I'd immediately contact the police and his first wife, and he could take the consequences.'

'And he agreed?' In spite of all he had told her, Caitlin still found it hard to believe that Roddy would be so easily defeated. She had thought he was dead once before, but he had come back from the grave!

Monro laughed shortly. 'He jumped at the proposition! Then he whined on about not having any money to go away with, and being chased by some villains who might kill him, so that he didn't even dare risk going back to wherever he had been living to pick up his possessions. Listening to his self-pitying complaints made me itch to kick his teeth in!'

'Yes, I know that mood of his . . . he must have been drinking to be so maudlin. But I do believe he's in trouble with some people he owes money to! I told you how he gambles and drinks, and from hints he dropped I think he has got involved in a drug racket over here.'

'I'm certain he has!' Monro said, his mouth hard and his grey eyes contemptuous. 'He was involved in drugs in South America, when he was there—in fact, my information is that that was how he got back to Europe. He was acting as a courier for drugs, bringing them into the country.'

'Oh, my God,' Caitlin whispered, her face white. 'As if things weren't bad enough, he had to get mixed up with something like that!'

'The detective agency picked up a vague rumour that he had stolen some of the drugs he brought in…either to use himself, or to sell. Hard to tell how much fire there was behind all the smoke, but if he did anything of the sort he's in very serious trouble. The kind of people he had got mixed up with never forgive that sort of pilfering. Criminals they might be, but they get quite incensed when anybody steals from them!' Monro's tone was sardonic.

'No wonder he's frightened!' Caitlin thought aloud, twisting the belt of her towelling robe round and round her hand while she stared at the floor. 'Poor Roddy.'

'Sorry for him?' Monro asked harshly, and she looked up in shock at the note in his voice.

'Stupid of me, I suppose, after the way he treated me, but maybe that's the difference between us. Roddy is never sorry for anyone. He would stamp anybody into the ground to gain an advantage, whereas I can't help feeling sorry for anyone in trouble. Even Roddy.'

Monro made a wry face. 'No, I know what you mean. I felt much the same. I couldn't stand listening to his whining any longer. I wanted to get rid of him fast, so I gave him an ultimatum, made him an offer he couldn't refuse!' He laughed roughly. 'So, today, someone from the detective agency will be putting him on to a plane back to South America, which seems far enough away from London and anyone who might be looking for him. Once there, he can do as he pleases, so long as he remembers never to come back here or get in my way again.'

'That was a very generous thing to do, considering that he'd tried to blackmail you,' Caitlin said gently. 'I hope he was grateful.'

Monro shrugged. 'Not that I noticed. In fact, he was full of complaints. He said he didn't want to go back to South America, so I said he needn't go to Mexico, he could try somewhere else this time. Then he said he would prefer Australia, but I told him Australia would never let him in! They stopped accepting criminals a long time ago. That made him furious, and he made some snide remarks about you, to get his own back——'

'About me?' She stiffened, not looking at him. 'What remarks?'

'They were meant to annoy me, and they succeeded!' Monro's jaw tightened, his face darkly flushed, his eyes seething with aggression. 'He was asking for a punch in the face, and he got one.'

'This was in the street? In Piccadilly Circus?'

Monro laughed, relaxing a little. 'No, we walked on into St James's Park from Piccadilly, and the only audience I had for the punch on the nose was a tramp sleeping under the trees nearby. He sat up and watched for a while, but as the fight was over in one punch he got bored and shambled off.'

'What did Roddy do?'

'Fell on the grass and refused to get up until he was sure I wouldn't hit him again. There was no blood, don't worry. He will probably have a black eye by now, that's all. When he did get to his feet I told him to make up his mind whether he was going to South America or staying here in police custody. Then he asked what he was supposed to do when he got there, since he didn't have any money at all. Was I going to give him some money, too? Or was he supposed to starve to death out there?'

She groaned. 'I'm so sorry! It's all my fault that he has caused you all this trouble. He has no sense of shame or gratitude, none of the decent human emotions.'

'He isn't your responsibility!' Monro gave her an impatient look. 'Try to remember that . . . you were never his wife and you aren't responsible for him in any way.'

'If it weren't for me you would never even have met him!'

Monro's mouth indented. He leaned back against the seat, his long brown legs gleaming in the sunlight. The dark hairs roughening their skin

had dried now, and so had his hair, tossed by a
light breeze. If she had seen him on a beach it
wouldn't have bothered her so much that he was
practically naked, but alone with her here on the
balcony of her suite it bothered her a great deal,
and she couldn't quite meet his eyes.

'I'm a pragmatist,' he drawled. 'And a realist!
I have met him, and I had to deal with the man.
It was obvious that the only way we could be sure
of getting rid of him was actually to put him on
to a plane going somewhere a long way off. He
didn't have the money for a ticket, but I did, and
it wasn't an amount I'd miss, so, although it irked
me to give him so much as a bent farthing, I decided that as I desired the end result I would have
to reluctantly accept the means necessary to
achieve it. And, as he claimed not to have any
money at all, I gave him enough cash to start a
new life with when he reached his destination,
and I assure you you've seen the last of Mr Roddy
Butler.'

'I hope you're right!' she sighed, and then they
both fell silent. There seemed nothing for them
to say to each other now that they had disposed
of the subject of Roddy Butler.

She was more uneasy in his presence than she
had ever been before during the whole time she
had known him. It was absurd. They had been
man and wife for two years, yet here she was
trembling, her stomach plunging in excitement,
just because he was a few feet away, wearing only
those black briefs, looking at her sideways with
what seemed to her like taunting mockery in his

grey eyes. What was he thinking? Why was he
watching her like that?

'One fact seems to have escaped your notice,'
he murmured.

Blankly, she stared back at him. 'What fact?'

'You are, after all, legally my wife,' he said
softly, and her body jerked in shock as that reg-
istered. She must have blanked out the realis-
ation until now, but it came home with piercing
emotion, and suddenly she was seeing everything
darkly, her eyes clouded over.

Monro gave an exclamation, looking up in
surprise, and Caitlin looked up too, only then
becoming aware that it wasn't emotion darkening her eyes at all. A bank of storm clouds had
arrived without either of them noticing it until
now. There was a rumble of thunder somewhere
and a splash of rain fell on Caitlin's face as she
turned it to the sky.

'Inside!' Monro said, getting to his feet. 'We're
about to have a real downpour.'

She ran for the french windows, with Monro
on her heels, and he pulled them shut after he
had joined her. They stood watching the rain
crash down in steely needles while the sky flashed
with lightning.

Caitlin shivered. 'That was sudden!'

'The weather can change suddenly here, but
this storm will pass quickly.'

She picked up the deliberate implication. He
was talking about more than just the weather.
He was telling her that life could go back to

normal now that Roddy was moving out of their sky, that all their troubles would soon be over.

But it wasn't that simple, was it? They might be legally married, after all, but their marriage had never been genuine. They had married for all the wrong reasons, and their marriage was totally unreal. She knew that the last few days had shown her the artificiality and emptiness of her marriage, and she could not go back to it.

'How's Gill?' she asked huskily.

'She misses you. You're an important part of her world now.'

She smiled sadly. 'I hope so, she's very important to me, and I've missed her every day.'

'I promised her we'd be back mid-week,' he said casually, standing just behind her so that she couldn't see his face. 'I have an important lunch on Wednesday, I'm afraid, but we can stay on here until that morning, and have the jet pick us up after breakfast. You obviously like it here. We could buy one of these suites and fly over from time to time, if you like.'

'I'm not coming back, Monro,' she said.

There was a silence, then he said quietly, 'What does that mean? You want a longer holiday? It must have been quite a strain on you, the last few days. I expect you need a long break, but——'

'I'm sorry,' she said desperately. 'That wasn't what I meant. I'm not ever coming back.'

He stiffened, his face grim, but as he opened his mouth to say something she rushed on huskily.

'I made a mistake in the first place, I should never have said I'd marry you. I should have stuck to my first reaction, and sent you away. Coming here has crystallised it all for me. Ever since we got married I've been like someone living inside a lovely landscape painting.' She paused, frowning as she searched for the right words to describe it to him, and Monro made a harsh, impatient sound.

'What are you talking about? You aren't making any sense.'

'I'm making sense to me, Monro! Listen... please, don't be angry, because there's no point. You've given me so much—you spoilt me, in fact, showered me with things, like that ruby necklace you gave me the other day. Millions of women would think I was crazy, being unhappy when everything surrounding me was perfect, harmonious—you have such beautiful homes, Monro, full of exquisite things. You have discreet and expert servants to take care of them. The best cars, furniture, antiques... yours is a wonderful world, and I've been living in it for the last two years in a positive dream. I didn't have to think, have to do anything very much, just drift about looking as if I belonged.'

'You did belong! You were my wife!' He was as tense as a coiled spring, and she was afraid he was going to leap at her any minute.

'No,' she said. 'No, Monro. Our marriage didn't have any depth, you must know that. I told you when you proposed to me that I didn't love you, but you insisted that it didn't matter.

And it did, Monro! It did, all the time. We just lived together, and sometimes shared a bed, although even that was less and less often as time went by...'

'You made it clear you didn't want me in your bed!' he grated.

She sighed wearily. 'Whatever the reason, Monro, the fact is...we weren't happy. Then Roddy came along and I had to step out of that frame into the real world, and I saw from the outside again, and real life is so different. Real life has sharp corners and knives that cut you, and ugliness, and poverty...but the fact that people bleed there means that they are alive, they aren't just dreamers drifting about in a daze. I can't go back, Monro. I want to be real. I want real emotions. I'd rather be hurt than not feel at all.'

She had turned to face him, her blue eyes wide and pleading, her delicate features pale. Monro stared down into her face, his own eyes hard, his brows drawn.

'Real emotions? Is that what you've been experiencing this weekend, with Joe Fanucci?'

The savagery of the question made her jump. 'Oh, for heaven's sake, Joe has nothing to do with what I'm talking about!'

'I'd say he has everything to do with it! Is he still here?'

'No, he flew back to London, and, anyway, I keep telling you, Joe is irrelevant——'

'Not to me! You left me and you went straight to him. You denied then that he meant anything to you. Just a friend, you said——'

'He is!'

He ignored that, his face set and darkly flushed, his mouth spitting out words like bullets from a machine-gun. 'But I find you over here in a cosy little apartment, and guess who's with you? Joe Fanucci again! And you still expect me to believe that he's just a good friend?'

'No, I don't expect you to believe anything I say. I've given up hoping you'll actually listen.'

'I'll listen—when you tell me the truth!' His face was stark, his bones angular under tight white skin; his eyes hated her.

'You aren't interested in the truth—only in what you want me to say. What exactly is it you want me to say?' She was now almost as angry as he was. They were shouting at each other, voices bitter. 'That I love Joe? OK, if that's what you want to hear—I love Joe!'

He lunged towards her suddenly, and she backed so quickly that she fell and sprawled, off balance, across one of the rugs. Monro was on top of her before she had a chance to pull herself together. His mouth searched for hers across her face as she tried to avert it. He finally caught her head between his hands and his mouth came down fiercely. Heaving and kicking under the force of his lean, naked body, she began to run out of air, suffocating and half fainting under that long, bruising kiss.

He pulled open her towelling robe, ripped the delicately made bikini top downwards, snapping the shoulder-straps, and his hands cupped her breasts as they spilled out, warm and smooth, glowing globes of flesh. Monro caressed slowly, breathing fast, his chest rising and falling visibly.

'You know you lied when you said I didn't want you,' he muttered thickly, lifting his head so that he could stare at her whole body, the towelling robe flung back, leaving her exposed, except where the tiny, delicate triangle of black silk covered her between the legs.

'Wanting isn't enough,' she whispered, both aroused and afraid of the way he made her feel.

'I've always wanted you, from the minute I first saw you,' he said, because he wasn't really listening to what she was trying to tell him. His hand swept down over her lingeringly. He undid the strings of the bikini bottom, so that she was utterly naked. He stared at her body, breathing in that hoarse way. 'Your body really drives me crazy,' he whispered, touching it slowly, tormenting her, and she shook, closing her eyes, pierced with intolerable desire.

He made a rough, satisfied sound and lay down on top of her, their bodies clinging breast to breast, belly to belly. He began kissing her again.

His mouth was hot and insistent, and deep inside her the aching began, the bittersweet need for his love that Monro didn't comprehend. He understood sex, and force, and desire. They were masculine words, imperatives which demanded only one female response: surrender. But he didn't know what love meant. He had never said, 'I love you', not once, and she was sure he never would.

His knee suddenly began pushing in between her legs, and panic darted through her. She gave a cry of angry protest, and tried to hit him, balling her hand into a fist. He caught her wrist and pulled her hand down, scowling blackly at her.

'I'm not giving you up to Joe Fanucci! You're mine, and I'll keep on reminding you of that until you understand!'

'I understand now. You think you bought me——'

His face went oddly white. 'I don't think anything of the sort! Are you trying to insult me?' He had let go of her, though, and she was able to sit up and pull the towelling robe around her again, tying the belt tightly to hide her nakedness.

'I'm just trying to get to the truth!' she said wearily.

He watched her, his eyes glittering. 'The truth? OK, you said you wanted some real emotion— well, the way I want you is real. How much more real do you want it?'

'That's the whole problem, Monro. You don't know. When you asked me to marry you, it was only because I wouldn't sleep with you otherwise, and you're so used to getting your own way that you couldn't stand it when someone actually said no to you. It made you absolutely determined to get me, come what may. Well, you married me, and you could sleep with me any

time you felt like it, and you lost interest then,
because that was your one and only objective all
the time—just to get me into bed. Once you had
achieved that, there was nothing left. Our marriage has been one long nothing.'

He frowned. 'If it has, it was because you
weren't interested in making anything of our
marriage! Oh, yes, you let me sleep with you—
but it was like sleeping with a dummy in a shop
window. You lay there looking beautiful and you
put up with my lovemaking, but you never let it
touch you, did you? You didn't enjoy it.'

'Are you saying I'm frigid?' That touched her
to the quick and she slowly flushed. 'That's a lie!
Why, just now——' She broke off, realising it
would be a piece of folly to let him know how
much she had wanted him just now.

'Yes,' he said with icy mockery. 'Just now, for
instance . . . you almost let go, didn't you? You
were getting quite excited there for a minute, and
I thought at last you were going to respond the
way I've always believed you could . . . and then
you went cold on me again, but you were afraid
you wouldn't be able to stop me this time, so you
fell back on hitting me to make me stop. That
was how it always was in bed with you, Caitlin.
You always made me feel I was raping you. In
the end, I couldn't stand that look of distaste on
your face. You froze me out of your bed, Caitlin,
so don't try to blame me for whatever went wrong
with our marriage. I wanted to make the marriage work. You refused to try. You wouldn't let
me near you.'

'No, that isn't true! I didn't ... I ...' She began to stammer and then fell silent, biting her inner lip. Was it true? Had she refused to let him near her? Had she been so cold towards him that she had driven him away? Well, in a sense, perhaps, she conceded reluctantly. But only because she knew he didn't care anything for her, because their marriage was a sham, a hollow shell. Even those nights when he had shared her bed, she had always sensed that he didn't feel anything but desire for her body.

'But you're going to start trying now!' Monro told her with angry insistence. 'You're coming back with me to London and you're going to make our marriage work. You aren't walking away from me or Gill—or from this marriage, Caitlin.'

'No,' she said sharply, facing him, her hands clenched at her sides, her chin up and her face flushed. 'I'm not coming back, because our marriage is a sham. You say I'm cold—what about you? You never made love to me! You took me! We had sex. But there was no love involved, and I don't want that sort of marriage any more. I want a divorce, Monro.'

'I'll never give you one!'

'A separation, then—legal or otherwise. I am leaving you, so you might as well give me a separation.'

'And how do you plan to support yourself?' he sneered. 'You've learnt expensive tastes, my dear.' He waved a hand around the elegant suite. 'This place, for instance! You've learnt to expect the best, but that costs money. You're expecting me to keep you, of course! Well, let me tell you——'

'No,' she interrupted sharply. 'I'll keep myself, thank you!'

'Oh, yes?' His brows arched sardonically. 'And how will you do that, exactly?'

'I shall get a job.'

He laughed icily. 'As a model? You're past it, far too old.'

If he expected the brutality of that truth to wound her, he was mistaken, and she gave him a level, scornful stare which made him move restlessly, frowning. 'I know I'm too old for modelling now,' she said. 'I'm going into the other side of the fashion business—selling! I'm going to train as a junior *vendeuse*.'

'In a fashion house?' His eyes narrowed, brilliant with rage and suspicion. His mouth twisted cynically. 'I wonder if I can guess whose fashion house you'll be joining.'

She didn't answer, staring at him defiantly.

'I thought so!' he bit out. 'You're leaving me to go to him, in fact! Yet you keep insisting that you're just good friends? You must think I'm really stupid if you expect me to believe you.' Monro walked away to the door. 'If you go to live with Joe Fanucci, I warn you—I'll destroy him! Think twice before you risk making me really angry, Caitlin.'

She followed halfway across the room, her face disturbed. 'Don't threaten me, Monro! What do you mean, you'll destroy Joe? Are you making threats against his life? For God's sake, you don't expect me to take that seriously?'

'His life?' Monro laughed coldly. 'No, no. I don't play those games. That is more Roddy Butler's style. I'm not threatening Joe Fanucci's life. I'm threatening his business. Credit is his life-blood. He's very successful, but he has a frequent cash-flow problem. Customers don't pay his bills. Some eventually do, others default. He has to borrow a lot of money to see him through until he gets more of the outstanding debt in . . . He banks with me.'

'Joe does?' Startled, she stared at him. 'He never mentioned that to me!'

'I don't suppose he is even aware of the fact. I haven't owned this particular merchant bank long. Just a couple of years, in fact. Since I married you. It was a logical progression, to acquire our own bank, just as we have our captive insurance company——'

'Captive insurance company?' she repeated blankly.

'Just a jargon word for an insurance scheme set up by a very big company,' he dismissed. 'Anyway, it was decided we ought to add a merchant bank to our list of companies, so we bought into this one, and lately I discovered that Fanucci banks with them. I noticed his name on a list of big debtors.'

Caitlin took a sharp breath. 'Big debtors? Joe? But he's very successful!'

'I told you—cash-flow is his problem, and the fact that his own creditors don't pay too readily.

I don't know what his overdraft is, to the last decimal point, but it's big enough, so that if I squeeze just a little I'll crush him.'

Caitlin looked at him with horror and scorn. 'You bastard.'

Monro's face tightened. He opened the door. 'Think about it, Caitlin. If you go to him, I'll ruin him, I promise you that.'

CHAPTER EIGHT

CAITLIN locked the door behind Monro, hating him. He was utterly ruthless; he would use any weapon that came to hand. Well, he wasn't browbeating, or coaxing, or blackmailing her this time. She remembered only too vividly how he had manoeuvred and manipulated to get her to marry him in the first place. He had even used his little girl, when he'd realised she was a useful weapon he held. He talked so scornfully of Roddy—where was the difference in their methods?

She was relieved to be rid of Roddy for good this time, of course. Monro had dealt with that with his usual cool efficiency. It hadn't even occurred to her that Roddy might have been married before—but it should have done. He wouldn't come back into her life, at least; she could be sure of that. She would just have to yell for a policeman and he would be in prison for bigamy before his feet had touched the ground, and he knew it.

Her mind absorbed in processing everything Monro had said to her, she walked slowly into the bathroom to shower before getting dressed. As she was towelling herself afterwards she caught sight of her naked body reflected in the bathroom mirror, and frowned at the shadowy bruises on her pale skin, where Monro's hard fingers had gripped her. He had left the mark of his desire imprinted on her flesh, and she turned away, shuddering.

She ought to be grateful to him for dealing with Roddy. He had lifted a terrible burden from her; she had been aghast at the thought that she was still Roddy's wife and that he was going to leech on to her for as long as he could get money out of her. It wasn't just the blackmail, though. Roddy knew such unpleasant people; he could have turned her life into a living hell, as he had before. She covered her face with her hands, sick with the memory.

Roddy would have sold her to one or other of his loathsome friends, if he could. She had been in dread of rape during the last weeks before the earthquake. It had been so terrifying to be in that strange country, alone, with a man like that. It had left indelible scars on her mind.

Were they the real reason why her marriage to Monro had never worked? she wondered suddenly, then walked quickly into the bedroom to dress, pushing that thought aside.

She chose a simple shift dress in crisp poplin, in pastel shades of pink and grey. Wearing it made her feel more in control, and the short sleeves hid the bruises on her shoulders and upper arms where Monro had forced her down against the floor while he'd kissed her so brutally.

No, Monro was the reason why her marriage hadn't worked out! If he had ever really shown her tenderness...

Her mind conjured up pictures from the past two years, and she frowned.

There had been moments, it was undeniable...

When they had been skiing in Gstaad and she had taken a tumble, Monro had been at her side in seconds, his face pale, gently touching her arms and legs to see what damage had been done. When he'd realised that she had slightly sprained an ankle, he had insisted on carrying her back to the hotel, and had stayed at her side instead of going out on the slopes himself, until her ankle had healed.

And she could remember during the first months together, waking up in the mornings to find him leaning on an elbow beside her, his head propped on his hand, just watching her sleeping. It had always made her uneasy; she had usually frowned, wondering what he'd been thinking about, and hating the thought of him staring at her while she'd been unaware of him.

She had blurted out something of the sort, she remembered, and since then she couldn't remember waking up to find him watching her.

She stared at herself in the dressing-table mirror, clipping imitation pearl studs into her ears, her hands shaky. Had she been gradually freezing him out of her life, then? Was he right?

She thought of all the presents he had given her, not merely the valuable jewellery, which she had always taken to be something like a badge of office, and which she had left behind without regret. Mrs Monro Ritchie had to be seen wearing good jewellery. The way she looked in public reflected on her husband; she was a living symbol and emblem. Caitlin had always resented it, but that had been unfair of her because it wasn't Monro's fault. He hadn't invented society's rules.

He was always giving her things, though. He was a very generous man, but she had never asked herself why—she had dismissed the presents as automatic tokens from a very wealthy man. But you couldn't say that of most of the things he'd brought her—like the little bunch of violets he had bought one evening, from an old woman outside a theatre they had been visiting. He had dropped it in her lap as they had sat down in their box, and all evening she had breathed the wild, sweet fragrance. When they had left she had pinned the violets to her white satin evening dress, and on the way home, in the back of the Rolls, Monro had bent to inhale the scent of the flowers, his mouth softly brushing the warm white flesh above the deep neckline of her dress.

She shivered, closing her eyes. Maybe he had shown her tenderness now and then—but one thing was certain. He had never told her he loved her; never even hinted at it. He had shown her every other aspect of passion from jealous rage to burning desire, but he had never, ever, said, 'I love you.' If he did love her, he would have said so.

Suddenly she stiffened, hearing someone trying the door of the suite. There was a pause, then the bell was pressed, loudly, insistently.

She gave her mirror a last, assessing glance. She looked cool and assured. Nobody who saw her would ever suspect that under her calm surface she was torn and divided; a battleground for opposing forces with the victory going first one way and then another, and no final outcome in sight.

She walked to the door and opened it, and Monro looked down into her face, his eyes searching.

'I was just going to lunch,' she said.

'I came to escort you over to the main building.'

'I hope we're not too late, though. It is nearly two o'clock.'

'They don't stop serving lunch until four. This is Spain, remember. Meals tend to be eaten much later here than they do in England.'

'Yes, that's true; I had forgotten.'

She closed the door behind her and they walked through the tropical gardens to the hotel, sunlight shifting down through the palm trees, illuminating their faces as they talked. They were both very polite, very careful, neither of them wanting another violent scene.

Over the lunch table she kept sneaking glances at him and hurriedly looking away, because she felt a melancholy familiarity in the way they were treating each other so courteously, so remotely. This was how it had been for a long time, and she could not live like this any more.

'You aren't eating,' he said, looking at her plate, which he had filled for her at the buffet table. He had chosen all her favourite food, and now he frowned. 'Would you rather have something else?'

'No, it's very good, but I'm not hungry.'

'Perhaps that's the heat,' he suggested, looking concerned. 'With your fair skin you shouldn't be out in the sun for long. You do look rather pale.'

He walked her back to her suite and she halted on the threshold. 'Well, I think I'll take a siesta now.'

'Good idea,' he said. 'I thought we might have dinner in Marbella tonight—or would you rather go to the club next door? Or Puerto Banus?'

She put a hand to her head, frowning. 'I can't even think of eating at the moment. I've got a headache, and I really do need some sleep.'

He inclined his head, his grey eyes cool, and walked away. She locked the door and went into her bedroom, stripped off and put on a cool cotton nightshirt which came just to her knees.

She was asleep minutes after closing her eyes, and her dreams were disturbing. She dreamt of Roddy and the earthquake, and was terrified; then she was sleeping deeply again, only to drift into another dream, even more real this time. She was with Monro and he was nearly naked, as he had been that morning, in his brief black swimming-trunks. His hands were touching her, warm and caressing, sliding under her nightshirt, pushing it up until she was naked, too. An intense wave of erotic pleasure swamped her; she moaned and clung to him, feeling the coolness of his skin against her own, the muscled power of his chest, his thigh.

His mouth moved down against hers, a warm, lazy, coaxing sweetness in the way he kissed her, in the gentle stroking of his hands. Caitlin was dizzy with sensuality, she had never felt anything like this feeling, and she felt no barriers, no fears, nothing to stop her from doing whatever she wanted to do.

She felt light pressing against her lids, her mind was being dragged up from the depth of sleep and she fought against waking. She did not want to stop this dream. Her body was burning with desire; she was so hot she felt as if she would set light to the bed. She tossed and twisted on the sheet, groaning, this piercing sensation deep inside her, and all the time something tried to wake her, something beat upon her brain.

Then it had stopped and she could slip back into the sweetness of the dream. Her arms were around Monro's neck and she moved against him, incited him, saw the passion in his eyes.

'Caitlin!' he said loudly, and he sounded anxious, not passionate. He was shaking her, not kissing her, and she hung limply between his hands, her blonde hair tumbling down her back, and reluctantly opened her eyes at last.

For a second she was confused—was she still dreaming? Was Monro in her dream—or really here?

'Monro? Are you in my dream, or am I awake?' she mumbled, but her brain was slowly starting to work. Really here, she thought dazedly. Monro is really here, in my bedroom, kneeling on the bed, his hands holding me, shaking me. In the dream he wasn't shaking me. He was doing something intensely more pleasurable, and she smiled drowsily, in reminiscence.

He was staring down at her, his brows a jagged line above his stabbing grey eyes. 'Are you awake? Or feverish?' he demanded, and she came fully awake, looking angrily at him.

'What are you doing in my room? I locked the door, I know I did. How did you get in here?'

'I have another key,' he said coolly.

Her eyes opened wider, and she looked furiously at him. 'What did you say?'

'I am your husband, after all, so the desk clerk supplied me with the second key to this suite.'

'He had no business doing that!'

'He knew we were married!'

'How could he be sure you weren't lying?' she burst out childishly, and Monro gave her a wry glance.

'Of course he knew who I was . . . and who you were. Our passports, remember? And, after all, we both have well-known faces! It never entered his head that you might object if I had the spare key. After all, I am your husband!'

'For the moment,' she said icily. 'Well, you can give the key to me. I won't have you walking in and out of here without knocking.'

'I knocked and rang, but there was no reply, and I got worried about you. You had looked so pale over lunch, I thought you might be ill.'

'I'm fine. I was fast asleep, that's all, until you broke in here and woke me up!'

'Fast asleep, and dreaming,' he said softly.

A tide of burning red flowed up her face as she remembered those dreams. She couldn't meet his eyes; her lashes fell and she gave him a disturbed look through them. Why had he mentioned dreaming? And in that voice? He couldn't know what she had been dreaming about—or could he?

She had hated it when she had woken up on those other occasions to find him leaning over her, watching her while she slept. Some atavistic instinct had made her dread the idea of being observed while she was so vulnerable. In sleep the conscious mind relaxed and the unconscious had control—but what if the face betrayed what was happening in the sleeping mind? What if her body movements had given her away to him? What if he had been able to see into her dream, and know what was happening in it?

'You still haven't told me why you're here,' she said, to distract him and to cover her own embarrassment. 'What time is it? Have I been asleep long?'

'Only an hour,' he said. 'But I had an urgent phone-call from London—Gill has got chicken-pox.'

She sat up with a worried cry. 'Oh, poor little Gilly. But why didn't they let us know earlier? How long has she been ill?'

'She had what I thought was a bad cold for several days, with a touch of temperature, but the spots have just appeared and the doctor diagnoses chicken-pox.'

'I can't remember...is that serious?' Caitlin asked, face anxious, and he smiled at her, shaking his head.

'Not normally, I gather, although Mrs Day says Gill keeps trying to scratch her face.'

'Has Mrs Day put mittens on her? She could be disfigured for life if she scratches the spots off.'

'You can make sure of that when you get there. I've asked my pilot to come at once to pick us up and take us home,' he said.

Us? She looked sharply at him, biting her lip, but he seemed unaware of her expression. He went on talking in a cool, confident voice.

'He'll be here in the jet in three hours. I'd given him a day off while I was here, so he has to get to the airfield and register his flight path before he can take off.'

He was taking it for granted that she would come, and she had to admit that she wanted to go. She wanted to be with Gill. Gill would need her. She did so hate being ill, all children did; she would be crying and fidgeting in the bed, driving her nanny mad, and, although Mrs Day was utterly devoted to Gill and always patient and long-suffering with her, Caitlin knew Gill would be waiting for her to come. She was Gill's mummy now. Gill called her Caitlin mostly, but they both knew that she had taken the place of the child's dead mother, both legally and in Gill's heart. If she didn't come when Gill needed her, what hurt would that inflict, what emotional damage would it do? She couldn't risk that.

She met Monro's eyes and saw the watchfulness in them. He was not so certain of her as he was pretending to be. A little tic beat beside his eye. Somehow, noticing that made her feel rather better.

'It won't take me long to pack,' she said flatly.

'I've already packed,' he said, 'I'll help you.'

She caught the note of satisfaction in his voice and froze in the act of swinging her legs off the bed, glaring at him.

'I'm coming back for Gill's sake!' she threw at him.

'But you're coming,' he flung back, his mouth hardening. 'And you're staying. You will not be taking that job with Fanucci. You'll stay where you belong in future, in my house.'

'I don't belong to you!'

His face set like stone. 'Yes,' he said thickly. 'You do, and it's time I proved it to you.'

He caught hold of her and flung her back across the bed. She gave a cry of fear that was strangled in her throat as he began kissing her with relentless force, bruising her lips back upon her teeth.

His hands were under her nightshirt; she tried to push them away, escape that intrusive intimacy, but although she was angry with him she couldn't stop the shivers of aroused desire running through her, making her skin icy, her teeth chatter in a shock of intense passion.

He had woken her from a dream where they made love; the reality and the dream merged helplessly inside her and she was hot and cold, her lips parting for him. She might fight him, but how could she fight herself? Her mind might have reasons for refusing him, but her heart had other reasons for needing what he was doing.

He was kissing her differently now; not with brutality, but coaxing her with deep, seductive kisses that teased and incited, until she was trembling and groaning, her arms around him and her body yielding.

Her eyes wouldn't stay open, she was slipping back into that dream, drifting on a tide of sexual yearning which swept her away. She began making love to him as she had in the dream. She caressed his neck and shoulders, her hands trembling with passion; she clung to him, kissing his mouth, his throat, his deep, tanned chest.

Monro seemed stunned; he just lay there, while she took the initiative, but his heart was crashing inside his chest, his lungs snatching air as if he was breathless.

She could hear the hoarse drag of his breathing as her head moved lower, her mouth exploring his body with an abandonment she had never risked before.

If she had not dreamt of this such a short time ago, she would never have dared; but, as in her dream, suddenly all things seemed possible. She was blind to everything but her own desire. She let her tongue taste him, and Monro gave a sudden groan, deep and hoarse. 'Darling,' he moaned. 'Oh, darling...'

She felt a stab of excitement. It gave her a sense of power to know she could do this to him, drive him out of his mind, his body twisting restlessly on the bed, his flesh hot and hard as she caressed it.

'Now, Caitlin,' he muttered, reaching for her and trying to push her down on her back. 'Darling, I want you so much it hurts. Now, darling...'

She made him wait, torturing him with prolonged and piercing sensuality; knowing just what she was doing and hearing his groans with satisfaction. For once she was the one who controlled what happened, and she was in no hurry to end her enjoyment. In all their previous love-making Monro had dictated what happened; she had just been quiescent, submissive, and at first that was all she had wanted to be because she had not loved him, but as she had begun to fall in love with him she had begun to long to express her feelings. She never had until now because she had been too embarrassed, too shy, and afraid of letting him see how she felt. But in this dreamlike state, suddenly she was free to take what she wanted, do as she pleased.

'Caitlin, for God's sake,' he moaned, his head moving from side to side on the pillow as she went on teasing him without allowing him to satisfy that primitive need. 'Now, darling, please, stop playing with me...'

'I like playing with you,' she whispered huskily. 'I don't want to stop.' Once he entered her she was afraid he would drive insistently to his own satisfaction, and it would all be over, too soon.

'It will be better, when we do make love; you'll see. You'll want it more.'

'I want it now,' he groaned, and she arched over him, laughing softly.

'Do you? Show me, then. This time you aren't just taking me, Monro, this time I want to enjoy it too. I want you to please me, first.'

His brows came together. 'Haven't you enjoyed it all the other times? Is that what you're saying?'

'You're always in too much of a hurry,' she said, moving her naked body softly against his, brushing her face against him, her lashes fluttering up and down on his skin. 'I don't just want sex, Monro. That is over too soon. The real pleasure comes before the sex, anticipating it.'

His eyes suddenly froze over. 'Does it now? And who taught you that since I last went to bed with you?'

She looked impatiently at him. 'Nobody, don't be stupid!'

'You must think I am stupid, if you don't expect me to work out the obvious—you've suddenly become an expert in bed and you must have had a teacher!' He was white, his eyes bitterly angry. 'Fanucci, of course! Who else could it be? I'll kill him, I'll kill him——'

'If you want our marriage to survive, Monro, you'd better start trusting me!' she shouted, wanting to hit him. 'I have never been to bed with Joe. Got that? Never. Never.'

He stared into her furious eyes, his brows drawn. 'If it isn't Fanucci, who *has* been teaching you?'

'My own needs,' she said fiercely, and saw his eyes widen. She nodded. 'Yes. I want you, but not the way you've always taken me before. I want you to start pleasing me, as well as yourself... or you can forget it!'

He began to laugh, lying back on the bed, shaking with amusement. 'Abandoned woman... is that an ultimatum?' Then his face changed, and she saw the alteration with a leap of the heart. 'I accept the terms,' he whispered. 'With pleasure.'

He lazily put out a hand to stroke her smooth breast, teasing the nipple until it hardened, his eyes moving hungrily over her body while she watched him, hardly able to breathe. During her months with Roddy she had been too young and inexperienced to know the refinements of love, the sweet torture of frustration which knew it would soon be satisfied. Since she had married Monro, she had been too busy defending herself, protecting herself from the pain of loving him, to give herself freely in bed. He was right. She had not wanted him in the beginning; he must always have felt that he was forcing himself on her unwilling body. That was why he didn't waste time in the preliminaries of love, but it would be different in the future.

She trembled, her body burning for him, pulling him down on her, and Monro made a deep, primitive sound, somewhere between a groan and a cry of hunger. His lean body slid between her parted legs and his hands explored her hot flesh.

'You're in a hurry,' she mocked, but Monro wasn't smiling any more. He was darkly flushed and urgent to take possession of her body. She heard the unsteady note of his breathing as he thrust into her at last.

She arched to meet his driving body, her arms and legs wound round him so that they were almost one flesh, galloping underneath him with a haste he matched, riding on her with relentless force.

The last time they had made love, Monro had taken his pleasure alone and left her unsatisfied and angry.

This time they climaxed together, their bodies shuddering and vibrating with the extremity of passion, cries of intense satisfaction throbbing in their throats.

'I love you,' she sobbed, heard herself say it, and was lost. She couldn't deny she loved him now, to herself or him. She couldn't call the words back or pretend she hadn't meant them, any more than she could stop the long drawn-out ecstasy shaking her whole body, or silence the moans of satisfaction she was giving.

Monro's arms tightened around her, and he made sounds of anguished pleasure, his face pushed hard against hers, his lips on her ear.

She couldn't hear what he was muttering, his body jerking and shaking on hers, but it didn't matter.

They lay still together, eyes closed, bodies damp with perspiration and trembling. Caitlin felt drowsy; she slowly fell into a light sleep, with Monro's dark head cradled on her breast, and he breathed regularly, as if he slept, too.

The sound of a car horn from the car park made them start, at last, their eyes opening. Monro stretched lazily, yawning, and sat up to lean on his elbow and stare down into her flushed face. Caitlin was self-conscious at once, her eyes moving away restlessly.

'Tell me again,' he said. 'Tell me you love me, my darling. I've waited so long to hear you say it, and I never thought I would.'

She smiled quiveringly, gave him a quick glance, her face shy. 'You never said it to me! Not once, all the time I've known you...not when you proposed, or when we were married.'

'Did I really have to say it? Why else do you think I married you? I fell in love with you the minute I saw your face on that magazine cover, and you've given me some very bad times over the years since then.'

'I'm sorry,' she said, pushing her face into his throat and kissing his skin.

'Mmm...that's nice,' he muttered, a hand wandering through her long blonde hair. 'I've wanted to tell you I love you a hundred times, but I didn't because I was afraid you would laugh at me, or look bored, or embarrassed. I hated the look on your face when I walked into your bedroom on the nights when we made love. You would go stiff and pale, and I knew you were hating everything I did. In the end, I stopped trying to make you love me, I stopped trying to seduce you. I stayed away from you for as long as I could stand it, and then I'd have to have you, but I made it fast, I never stayed long.'

'I know,' she said drily. 'You hurt me far more then. You just took me and satisfied yourself, then went out with hardly a word. I hated you.'

'I'm sorry. Oh, God, I'm sorry, Caitlin. If only you'd said something...'

'What could I say?' she asked, giving him a wry glance. 'Please, make love to me more slowly, because I think I'm beginning to want you, but not this way. This way is more like rape than love. Is that what I should have said? How could I?'

He groaned and picked up her hand, kissed it humbly, his mouth lingering in her warm palm. 'I'm sorry. We've wasted two years, and I've been a dumb fool...but I did love you, all the time, Caitlin, and I tried to show it without actually putting it into words that would just embarrass you. Be honest, now—if I had burst out with how I felt, how would you have reacted?'

She sighed, nodding. 'Neither of us has handled this very brightly, have we? I'm sorry, too, Monro. When I met you, I was still hurt and bitter, over Roddy, and I wasn't ready to fall in love again. I don't even know when I started to love you; I think I was trying to kid myself that it wasn't happening.'

'And still trying today,' he said, his mouth twisting. 'Or have you forgotten that you were going to leave me and go to work for Fanucci?'

She made a face. 'I didn't think I could bear living with you when I was so much in love but you didn't love me. I didn't want to get hurt again.' She closed her eyes, shivering. 'Just think... if Gill hadn't got chicken-pox we might have separated and never met again!'

Monro gave her a sideways smile of glinting mockery. 'You don't really think I was going to let you go, do you? If Gill hadn't got chicken-pox I'd have thought of some other way of keeping you. I told you, my darling, you're mine, and I am never going to let you out of my sight.'

Caitlin shook her head, her mouth curving teasingly, her blue eyes full of provocation. 'You've got that all wrong, Monro. *You* are mine. And I am never going to let you go.'

THIS JULY, HARLEQUIN OFFERS YOU THE PERFECT SUMMER READ!

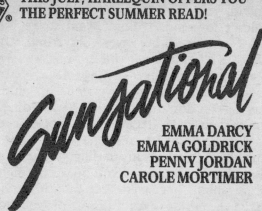

Sunsational

**EMMA DARCY
EMMA GOLDRICK
PENNY JORDAN
CAROLE MORTIMER**

From top authors of Harlequin Presents comes HARLEQUIN SUNSATIONAL, a four-stories-in-one book with 768 pages of romantic reading.

Written by such prolific Harlequin authors as Emma Darcy, Emma Goldrick, Penny Jordan and Carole Mortimer, HARLEQUIN SUNSATIONAL is the perfect summer companion to take along to the beach, cottage, on your dream destination or just for reading at home in the warm sunshine!

Don't miss this unique reading opportunity.

Available wherever Harlequin books are sold.

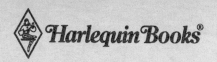 **Harlequin Books®**

GREAT NEWS...

HARLEQUIN UNVEILS NEW SHIPPING PLANS

For the convenience of customers, Harlequin has announced that Harlequin romances will now be available in stores at these convenient times each month*:

Harlequin Presents, American Romance, Historical, Intrigue:

> May titles: April 10
> June titles: May 8
> July titles: June 5
> August titles: July 10

Harlequin Romance, Superromance, Temptation, Regency Romance:

> May titles: April 24
> June titles: May 22
> July titles: June 19
> August titles: July 24

We hope this new schedule is convenient for you.

With only two trips each month to your local bookseller, you'll never miss any of your favorite authors!

*Please note: There may be slight variations in on-sale dates in your area due to differences in shipping and handling.

HDATES-R

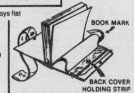

Back by Popular Demand

Janet Dailey
Americana

A romantic tour of America through fifty favorite Harlequin
Presents® novels, each set in a different state researched by
Janet and her husband, Bill. A journey of a lifetime in one
cherished collection.

In June, don't miss the sultry states featured in:

Title # 9 - FLORIDA
         Southern Nights
    #10 - GEORGIA
         Night of the Cotillion

Available wherever
Harlequin books are sold.